Silence again filled the room. Dawn wondered briefly if the two doctors realized that there was a moth flapping against the plate glass window behind them. She studied the insect as it flailed and beat its wings on the clear glass, desperate to touch the sun outside. *Poor moth . . .*

"This is not a decision for you to make right now, Dawn," Dr. Sinclair said, breaking the heavy silence. "Go home and think about it. Discuss it. But don't take too long. We'll need to proceed as soon as possible if you decide in favor of the procedure."

"The odds," Rob said. "What are the odds of the transplant succeeding?"

The two doctors exchanged quick glances. "Without it, Dawn has a twenty percent chance of survival. With it, fifty-fifty."

D1413400

I WANT TO LIVE

Lurlene McDaniel

SCHOLASTIC INC.

New York Toronto London Auckland Sydney
Mexico City New Delhi Hong Kong Buenos Aires

To Mark and Jenelle,
Tim and Todd.
Soli Deo Gloria.

No part of this publication may be reproduced in whole or in part, or stored in a retrieval system, or transmitted in any form or by any means, electronic, mechanical, photocopying, recording, or otherwise, without written permission of the publisher. For information regarding permission, write to Lerner Publications Company, a division of Lerner Publishing Group, 241 First Avenue North, Minneapolis, MN 55401.

ISBN 0-439-69210-5

Text copyright © 1987 by Lurlene McDaniel. All rights reserved.
For information contact Darby Creek Publishing, 7858 Industrial Parkway,
Plain City, OH 43064. Published by Scholastic Inc., 557 Broadway, New York, NY 10012,
by arrangement with Darby Creek Publishing and Lerner Publishing Group.
SCHOLASTIC and associated logos are trademarks and/or registered trademarks of Scholastic Inc.

12 11 10 9 8 7 6 5 4 3 2 1   4 5 6 7 8 9/0

Printed in the U.S.A.   01

First Scholastic printing, October 2004

Cover photo and design by Michael Petty, Petty Productions

One

THE one thing that Dawn Rochelle remembered most about her fourteenth birthday was that she was still alive. In her diary, she wrote:

March 23,

Well, I've made it for almost a whole year. It doesn't seem possible that I've had leukemia since last April. I wish this hadn't happened to me. I wish I didn't have to go to the clinic for my checkup next week. I wish they didn't have to poke a hole in my back and take my spinal fluid—what if they find cancer cells? I can't think about it.

Today at school I heard that Jake Macka is moving. I wonder what it would be like to have him kiss me. I wonder if any "normal" boy will ever kiss me.

For my birthday, Mom and Dad gave me a "boombox" in hot pink. Rob sent a Michigan State mug and a pink sweatsuit. He's coming home for spring break this Saturday and I can hardly wait to see him. He says he's got someone special for us to meet. I'll bet it's Darcy, the girl he was dating last Christmas.

Fourteen is all right, more than I thought I'd see when I was so sick in the hospital last year. But how about fifteen? Will I see fifteen?

Dawn looked over her neatly formed words. She had been in remission for almost one whole year. It had been one year since her hospitalization, the pain, the tubes in her chest and mouth, the IV bottles, the chemotherapy, the side effects from all the drugs. It was all mostly over with now. These days she went for checkups at the clinic twice a month where she received the medications, but in smaller doses. Her doctors called it "maintenance." Some of the worst was behind her. But the fear wasn't—the horrible fear that the leukemia would come back. And that it would kill her, as it had Sandy Chandler, her once and best friend.

She sighed and shut the purple cover of her diary. I'll write more in it later, she thought. She'd learned about keeping a diary from Sandy. She often felt that if she died, the diary was something special and personal her parents could keep.

"Happy Birthday!"

Dawn whirled around to the smiling face of Rhonda Watson from the school's cheerleading squad.

"Your mom was out front and said I could come on up. What's happening?" Rhonda bounced into the room. Her brown hair swirled over her shoulders as she flopped onto the bed.

"Nothing much," Dawn answered. "What's happening with you?"

"I brought you a present." She tossed a brightly wrapped box to Dawn.

"Gee, thanks." Dawn was surprised. Even though she and Rhonda had been on the cheerleading squad together for two years, she'd never thought of Rhonda as an especially close friend. They'd done their share of hanging around together after football games in the fall, but Rhonda had never gone out of her way during the rest of the school year to be Dawn's friend. And now, she'd brought a gift. Dawn tore off the paper. Pink tennis socks and a matching headband lay in the tissue. "Gosh, Rhonda. This is great! Thanks."

"Well, I heard you tell Kim that your brother sent you a pink sweatsuit." Rhonda fidgeted with the ruffle on the bed pillow. "Is—uh—Rob coming home for spring break?"

Suddenly, Dawn figured out what Rhonda was up to. "He's too old for you, Rhonda."

"I'm a very mature fifteen," Rhonda sniffed, her face flushing.

"Don't get all huffy, I'm just being honest with you," she said. "Rob's twenty-one and besides I think he's bringing home a special girl to meet the family."

Rhonda's expression fell. "Oh. Well, it never hurts to ask." She bounced off the bed and looked around the powder pink and white room. Her eyes stopped in front of the shelves of teddy bears. "I like your collection." She went over and picked up Mr. Ruggers. "Boy, he looks like he's been around forever."

The bear had been Dawn's first teddy when she was a baby. One glass eye was missing and his fuzz had been rubbed off in several places. Suddenly, she felt funny about Rhonda touching the raggedy old animal. She took

Mr. Ruggers and casually flipped him into a heap on the floor. "Yeah, he was an original from my baby shower. When I was a little kid, he was my favorite. He's nothin' but junk now."

Rhonda stepped over the bear and continued surveying the shelves. "I'll bet you have the best collection in Ohio."

"I'll bet I have the *only* collection in Ohio. I've been thinking about getting rid of them. I'd rather start collecting something more—" she wanted to say "grown-up," but settled on "meaningful."

"Don't do that. My dad used to collect baseball cards when he was a boy and he said he'd be a rich man today if he'd saved them all. You never can tell what's going to be valuable."

If I live that long, Dawn thought. She said, "Would you—uh—like a root beer or something?"

"Sure. I'm *dying* of thirst. Are you having a birthday party?"

Dying of thirst, Dawn thought, what a silly expression. "We're just having cupcakes tonight. We're saving the big cake and ice cream bash for when Rob's home." Dawn led the way down the stairs to the Pennsylvania Dutch style kitchen.

"You sure he has a girlfriend? I can act older than I am, you know."

Dawn giggled. "I've seen Darcy's picture. There's no hope, Rhonda."

"I'm too young for all the neat guys," Rhonda complained.

Dawn understood Rhonda's complaint. "Tell me about it. Who's interested in a fourteen-year-old with . . ." she stopped, feeling her cheeks burn. ". . . with no curves and bumps in the right places." *With cancer,* her brain said.

"Oh, I don't know . . . " Rhonda cut her eyes sideways at Dawn. "Sometimes it seems like Jake Macka's interested."

"He's cute, isn't he?"

"For a fifteen-year-old," Rhonda sniffed. "Personally, I prefer older men."

Dawn sloshed root beer on the table. "I have an uncle in his 40s . . ."

Rhonda stuck out her tongue. "I said 'older,' not ancient. So what's with you and Jake?"

"Nothing. He's been nice to me ever since . . . well, since I got sick. But he's never asked me out or anything."

"Are you okay now? I mean, since your hair's grown back and everything, I don't much think of you as sick."

No, Rhonda. I'm not okay. I'm in remission. Until I'm cancer-free for five years, I won't ever be okay. "Yeah, I'm doing all right." She watched Rhonda toy with her glass. "Are you doing anything special this summer?"

"Hanging around mostly. Mrs. Booth wants me to babysit her kids three mornings a week while she works. How about you?"

"Hanging around, too. I'll probably go to camp again."

"That cancer camp? The one you went to last year? Ugh. How can you stand being around all those sick kids?"

Rhonda's questions irritated Dawn. How could she explain that it was more than cancer camp and sick people? Maybe if Rhonda thought cute guys went, she'd act differently. "It's fun. I met a neat guy there last year. His name's Greg and he's a senior in high school in Cincinnati. He's on an important swim team, too. He may be in the Olympics someday. He writes me." Actually, Greg hadn't written since Christmas, but she wanted Rhonda to think otherwise.

Rhonda wrinkled her nose. "Well, I probably wouldn't like any kind of camp. I'm the indoor type." She glanced up at the kitchen wall clock. "Good grief. Look at the time. I told Mom I'd be home fifteen minutes ago."

Dawn forced aside her annoyance, walked Rhonda to the back door and watched her

11

scurry off across the newly greening back yard. The dog next door barked. The air still held a chill and Dawn hugged her arms to herself and shivered. What *would* it be like to return to camp? How many kids would really come back? Would Greg be there? Or Mike, Greg's friend who'd lost his leg to bone cancer? Sandy wouldn't. *Sandy. I miss you, Sandy . . .*

No, she could never explain to Rhonda that it was comforting to be around kids like herself. To have friends who understand about clinic visits and blood work and chemotherapy and constant nausea from medications. The Rhondas of the regular world would never know what it was like to walk between normal and abnormal. To balance between "well" and "sick." Or to be a kid who might die before she has ever had a chance to live.

Two

FOR Dawn, Saturday morning moved very slowly. She paced back and forth on the carpet. How long did it take Rob to drive from East Lansing anyway?

"Dawn, you're going to wear out the carpet," Mrs. Rochelle scolded her daughter gently. "He'll be here soon enough." She adjusted her half-frame glasses and continued her needle-point project.

"I know. Did he say anything to you all about this mystery person he wants us to meet?"

"He said that *she* lives in Toledo, that he'll be dropping her off at her home and then he'll come here."

Dawn thought, *So I was right. It is Darcy.* "Well when are we supposed to meet her?"

"Rob plans to spend some time with just the four of us. Then she'll drive here Thursday and they'll both stay here with us through the weekend. I thought I'd put her on the sleeper sofa in your father's den. Anyway, Rob will follow her back, spend a few days with her family, then they'll both return to campus in his car."

"Boy, Rob must like her a lot to hang around home on spring break. Last year he went to Daytona Beach."

Mrs. Rochelle laid down her sewing on the table. "It happens to everyone sooner or later, dear—even your brother."

"What happens?"

Mrs. Rochelle placed her hand over her heart, rolled her eyes and whispered, "True love."

Dawn giggled. "Oh, Mom . . ."

The honk of a car horn interrupted Dawn. She ran to the front door. Outside, Rob's silver-colored, battered old Toyota coasted to the curb. Dawn ran down the front walk and threw herself into her brother's arms as soon as he got out of the car. "Hey, Squirt. Watch out or you'll knock me over."

Dawn hugged him fiercely. Her cheek pressed against his sky-blue sweater. He smelled faintly of herbal scented aftershave. "What took you so long?"

Rob tousled her auburn hair and peered

down into her green eyes. "You look super, Squirt." His voice softened. "I guess I can't call you that too much longer. You're turning into a very pretty young lady."

She blushed and pushed away from him. "Oh, come on."

"You doubt the word of a man who's personally surveyed hundreds of girls? Who's in a better position to judge how pretty you're getting?"

Rob scooped Dawn up and tossed her head-first over his broad shoulder. Dawn squealed, dangling head down over his back. "Put me down, Rob Rochelle! Right this instant."

He carried her like a sack of potatoes onto the porch where their mother waited. "Put her down, son," Dawn heard her mother demand. Dawn's feet found the wooden flooring.

"I—I'm sorry, Mom, Dawn. For a minute there, I forgot. Did I hurt you?"

Dawn wiped her forehead and felt her bubbling good spirits disappear. She looked from Rob's stricken face to her mother's anxious expression. "Stop it," she demanded from both of them. "Stop acting like I'm going to break or something. I'm perfectly fine and I *hate* being treated like a freak!"

"That's not it at all, honey . . . " Mrs. Rochelle began.

"It is, too." Dawn interrupted. "Can't I have some fun with my own brother?"

"Of course, but because Rob's been away at school, he doesn't understand your condition completely."

"No one understands," Dawn snapped.

Rob reached out and put his big arms around his sister and mother. "Hey—Is this any kind of welcome home celebration? Don't you two start yelling at each other because I tossed Dawn around like a little kid. It's my fault." He squeezed Dawn tightly. "Mom's right. But it has nothing to do with your medical problems. You're growing up and I should treat you that way."

But Dawn knew that wasn't exactly true. Everything was different because she had cancer. "Forget it. You're home and tonight's my special birthday party. We saved the cake just for you."

"Just for me? Do I have to share?"

"You bet, buster," Mrs. Rochelle added, opening the front door and leading the way into the house. "These hips of mine have been begging for this cake for days. You wouldn't want to disappoint them, would you?"

Rob laughed. "Mom, you still have the shape of a movie star." He and Dawn exchanged mischievous glances before adding in unison,

"Miss Piggy's!"

"Ha-ha. Very funny."

The awkward feeling Dawn had had on the porch faded away. Sometimes the Rochelle family could forget the reality of cancer and be a normal family. Anyone looking on right now would never know the truth. Dawn snuggled close to Rob and smiled adoringly into his sparkling blue eyes.

Later that night, after supper and cake and ice cream, Dawn perched on the swing on her front porch, watching the sky turn from pale pink to deep lavender to midnight blue. The front door swung open. Rob came out and sat down so hard that the old wooden swing groaned and squeaked. "One of us weighs too much," he noted, casting a sidelong glance at Dawn.

"It can't be me," Dawn countered.

"You had two giant pieces of cake. Why I've seen two-hundred-pound football players eat less."

"Sometimes sweet things taste extra good to me. It's because of my chemotherapy, I think." She wished she could have bitten her tongue. The last thing she wanted to talk about with Rob was her illness.

"Mom says you go for your checkup at the clinic on Wednesday. Would it be okay if I went with you?"

Dawn was surprised at his request. She turned in the swing to see him, pulling her feet onto the seat and resting her back against the wooden side arm. "Why? It's a long boring day and all you'll have to do is sit and wait."

Lamplight from the living room spilled onto his shoulders and caused highlights to glimmer off the top of his brown hair. "It's something I've never done. Mom or Dad always go and because I've been away at school I don't feel like I've been much support to any of you."

"That's not true. You write and call me all the time . . . and you visited me in the hospital."

"Don't you want me to take you?"

Dawn clasped her knees to her chest. "Sometimes . . . after the treatment . . . well, I get sort of sick . . ."

He turned his face toward her and the lamplight shone on his rugged features. His eyes looked tender. "Do you think I've never seen anyone throw up before?"

Dawn became flustered. She didn't want to be sick in front of Rob. "They're going to do my spinal tap, too."

"Tell me exactly what they do to you."

"I go into the clinic for chemo twice a month. First, they take blood samples for a

18

white blood cell count, a hemoglobin, and a platelet count. Once a month they do a spinal. Once every six weeks they do a bone marrow aspiration."

"What's that?"

"Well they stick a needle into my hip bone and draw out some of my bone marrow to see if the chemotherapy is still working."

"Does it hurt?"

"Sometimes. Just a little," she added hastily when she saw his jaw tighten. "But so far my marrow's looking good and that means I'm still in remission. I don't mind."

They swung in silence for awhile, watching the evening stars twinkle like tiny Christmas tree lights. "You seem to know a lot about your illness," Rob said.

"I want to know everything I can about it. Mom and Dad made a pact with me when I was first diagnosed. 'No secrets.' They promised to share everything the doctors told them. In fact, Dr. Sinclair—he's the main specialist on my case—said he'd always be honest with me about every single aspect of my treatment. It isn't half as scary when you know what's happening to you. Or what to expect to happen."

"I don't blame you, sis. I'd want to know the truth if it were me."

Dawn picked a bit of lint off the knee of her jeans. "Kids aren't dumb, you know. After all, it's *my* disease. I have a right to know what they're going to do to me."

"That's one of the reasons I want to take you to the clinic. It's about time I knew more, too. We're family, Dawn, and I think you're the bravest person I've ever known."

Tears collected in her eyes, but she refused to let him know. Playfully, Dawn balled up her fist and punched him in the arm. "You're nothing but a big old teddy bear. How'd you get the reputation of being a big mean football star?"

"I have a good agent," he said, clearing his throat. Together they sat in silence until Dawn's eyelids began to droop. On Wednesday, Rob would take her to the clinic. *Let me have a good report,* she prayed silently. *Please God . . . let me have a good report.*

Three

"**G**OOD morning, Dawn. That shade of pink looks terrific on you—even if it is one of our hospital gowns. How's school? Ready for summer vacation?" The questions came from Leslie Hughes, the animated black-haired nurse in the Oncology Clinic of the Columbus Children's Hospital. Leslie made notations on Dawn's chart while a lab technician drew vials of blood from a needle inserted in her arm.

"I'm missing a history exam so I could come here today, but my teacher said I could make it up later."

"Who's that gorgeous man waiting for you in the reception area?"

Dawn flashed Leslie a wide smile. She scarcely noted the blood draining into the technician's syringes through the plastic tubing of her Heparin lock. The device had been inserted earlier into the vein of her arm to allow them to take blood and administer drugs without repeatedly sticking her with needles throughout the day. "That's Rob, my brother. He's home on spring break. He plays football for Michigan State. He's cute, huh?"

Leslie rolled her eyes. "I'll bet the girls stand in line to date him."

"Well someone in the family had to get good looks." She smoothed a wrinkle from the tape holding the tube in place on her skin.

"Dawn Rochelle! You're as cute as a button. Aren't you beating guys off with a stick?"

Guys don't fall all over girls with cancer, Mrs. Hughes, Dawn thought. "Ugh! Who's got time for boys?" she said, wrinkling her nose.

Leslie wrote more information on Dawn's report, flipped shut the silver cover of the clipboard and stood. "You will someday, Dawn dear. Now let's go down the hall for your lumbar puncture."

Dawn followed Leslie, her palms sweating. She hated the spinal tap the most of all. The resident doctor who did the procedure was very gentle, but it still always hurt. And afterward, she got the worst headache—even if she lie perfectly flat for thirty minutes as the doctor recommended.

"Hi, Dawn. How are we doing today?" the

resident greeted her warmly and helped her onto the stainless steel work table.

"Hi yourself." She hunched over while he parted the hospital gown and tapped along her backbone.

"Would you like to lie down or sit up?"

"I'd rather lie down." She curled up into a tight ball, grasping her knees firmly to her chest.

"You know I'll do my best not to hurt you."

"I know."

Leslie helped hold her in position because it was crucial that she remain absolutely still during the process. Dawn felt the cool spray of a local skin anesthetic on her warm flesh. She shivered. She sensed, rather than felt the needle slide through her lower back, between her boney vertebrae and into the fluid space of her spinal column. She felt pressure, then pain. Dawn squeezed her eyes shut, using the technique of *imaging* they'd taught her in the early days of her first hospital admission.

She pictured herself walking through fields of softly blowing wildflowers. She imagined summer scents of gardenia and jasmine and breezes fluttering on her skin. In the center of the field, someone waited for her. Someone tall with deep brown eyes. *Was it Jake Macka?* Dawn's eyes flew open. Her fantasy was replaced by the reality of the clinic walls. *Stupid choice,* she said to herself.

"We're all finished." Dawn heard the resident say and felt Leslie relax her grip. Slowly, she uncurled and rolled onto her back. *Lie still,* she told her body. *If I lie perfectly still, maybe I won't get a headache this time.*

Leslie leaned over and patted her face. "You handled that beautifully, Dawn. Why don't you lie here for awhile and then I'll come back and we'll set up your chemo IV's."

"Sure." Dawn said and closed her eyes.

She did not have a headache when Leslie walked her down the hall to the chemo room after lunch. The room was painted a tranquil pale blue. It contained several cushioned chairs that looked like dental chairs. Beside each chair stood a metal IV stand.

Dawn settled into a chair. Leslie flipped the plastic bag containing Dawn's prescribed dose of medications on a hook at the top of the stand. She inserted a needle into the bag and another into Dawn's Heparin lock device. Then she adjusted the flow of the drip with a special clamp along the tubing. "That looks about right. Comfy?"

Dawn watched as the cancer-fighting chemicals slowly dripped down the tube toward her vein. "Is Rob doing all right in the waiting area?"

"I checked on him earlier and sent him out to have lunch. Want me to have him come back and visit with you?"

"No," Dawn said quickly. Even though he had offered to be a part of her treatment, she didn't want him to see her all hooked up to tubes and needles.

"Joan Clark passed by earlier and asked if you were planning on going back to camp this summer."

"Absolutely," Dawn said, remembering the play therapist who'd talked her into attending camp the previous summer. "I had the best time of my life at that camp. And met some great kids there."

Leslie's brow puckered, "I'm told some good-looking boys attend. Is there someone special you're anxious to see?"

Dawn felt her cheeks grow warm. She remembered Greg and his kiss by the lake. Her first kiss. Her *only* kiss. "Don't be silly. I just want to have a good time, that's all." Camp had been the only "fun" thing her disease had brought her. Besides, she *had* to return. Hadn't Sandy trusted her ashes from the bonfire to Dawn? If Dawn didn't take them back, who would?

Leslie handed her a magazine and glanced

at her wristwatch. "I'd love to dig the details out of you, Miss Rochelle, but duty calls." Dawn watched her scurry away to other patients and sighed. *Two hours,* she thought grudgingly. Two hours of sitting and thinking while the medicines seeped into her blood. She hoped Rob wasn't going crazy in the waiting room.

Dawn thought about Darcy. She remembered a pretty-faced girl with cascades of thick, blond hair from a photograph. "I hope you appreciate my brother," she whispered to herself. "I hope you know how lucky you are to get a guy like him." The chemicals dripped steadily through the tube. Dawn closed her eyes and imagined that the chemicals were prowling her blood like secret police, finding and destroying any cancer cells that might be lurking in her body.

When the long day was over, Rob piled her in the car, chatting about a little boy who dropped an ice cream cone on his sneakers. Dawn leaned against the seat, half-listening. She felt shaky. *Let me make it home,* she begged silently. But she had to tell Rob to stop the car along the side of the road, where she leaned out the open door and gagged and heaved. Rob held her hand and said soothing words. He rubbed her neck and smoothed her forehead until the vomiting stopped enough to go the rest of the way home.

Rob carried her up the stairs and tucked her under her covers. Then he put a cool cloth on her forehead. "Are you going to be all right?" he asked.

"Of course." Her voice was barely a whisper. "Thanks, Rob. Thanks for everything."

"I didn't do anything but sit and wait, Squirt. I'd give anything if I could do more. Anything."

Dawn attempted a smile. "Please don't share all the details with Darcy. No use scaring her off."

He stroked her cheek and said, "You couldn't scare anybody off. And Darcy's pretty tough to put up with someone like me. Now stop your chattering and go to sleep."

"I'll be better in the morning, Rob. I promise."

He paused at her bedroom door and asked, "I know this is a silly question, but would you like that teddy bear of yours? The scruffy-looking one—Mr. Ruggers?"

"I'm too old for teddy bears."

It was a long time before she heard Rob answer. His voice was so soft she almost didn't make out his words. He said, "You're never too old for teddy bears, Dawn. You're just too young for cancer."

Four

DAWN dressed in pink jeans and a bright flowered sweatshirt. She brushed her auburn hair into a barrett, glad that it had almost grown back to normal. A light dusting of blusher and a dash of pink lip gloss completed her image. For reasons she didn't understand, she wanted to look her absolute best when she met Darcy Collin.

It was noon before Darcy's car coasted into their driveway. Rob bounded down the walk and across the sunwarmed grass to open the car door. Darcy scooted out and sprang into his arms. Dawn watched them hug.

"Come meet my favorite 'other woman,'" she heard Rob say. Dawn approached shyly and nervously. She felt every bit like a gangling fourteen-year-old kid staring at a fairy princess. Darcy's hair hung in thick cascades the color of cornsilk. She wore a pastel sky-blue outfit that matched her eyes exactly. Her ivory face was smooth and enhanced by soft pink highlights. A gold chain nestled at her throat.

"Hello, Dawn. Rob's told me so much about you. How pretty you are." Darcy's hand was fine-boned and delicate. Dawn touched it gingerly.

Beside Rob, Darcy seemed tiny as she snuggled into the hollow of his arm. "Nice to meet you, too," Dawn mumbled.

Her parents appeared and another round of introductions occurred. Finally, they went inside the house.

"It's so good to finally meet you all. Rob wanted me to come over Christmas." Darcy explained in the cozy kitchen as the family sipped tea and nibbled on homemade chocolate chip cookies. "But we were in Aspen skiing."

Dawn slipped Rob a sidelong glance. *Skiing in Aspen?* He winked sheepishly. Dawn remembered Debbie, Rob's girlfriend through high school. Simple, bubbly, with brown hair, a smattering of freckles and a big, open smile. Girls like Darcy came from a different universe.

"What's your area of interest at college?" Mr. Rochelle asked, stirring his tea. Dawn noted that her mom had put out the good china even for the informal get-together.

"You mean besides me?" Rob quipped.

Darcy flashed him a smile and Dawn saw straight white, perfectly even teeth. "I'm majoring in communications—television actually. I've always wanted to work on-camera."

"As a news anchor?" Mrs. Rochelle asked.

"Maybe. I'm also studying journalism."

"Don't you think she'd make a great sportscaster? All the men would tune in just to watch her read the scores."

Darcy punched Rob playfully. "I'd like to think they'd tune in because of my ability, not my looks."

"With your looks, who needs ability?"

Everyone but Dawn laughed. She felt left out. And that made her feel guilty. Later, when Rob carried Darcy's things into the den, Dawn started up the stairs. But Darcy stopped her. "Just a minute, Dawn. I have something for you."

Hesitantly, Dawn entered the room where Darcy was rummaging through her suitcase. "Now where is that box? Here it is. I hope you like it." She held out a silver foil-wrapped gift with a baby-blue bow.

Dawn fumbled with the paper. "Thanks.

You didn't have to get me a present." Inside was a fist-sized teddy bear made of crystal. Dawn cupped it in her palm.

"Rob said you collected them," Darcy explained. "I hope you don't have another like it."

Dawn shook her head. Her shelves were full of fluffy, stuffed, inexpensive teddys. "I—I . . . it's beautiful." Sunlight shimmered through the chiseled glass, sending rainbows of light around the room.

"I'm glad you like it." Darcy smiled quickly and then turned to finish unpacking. "I hope we can get to know each other better and become friends."

"Ah—sure. That's what I'd like, too." She watched for a few awkward moments while Darcy hung her clothes on hangers.

"I had no idea what Rob might want to do, so I brought one of everything in my closet. When we go back to my house my parents have planned this big party . . ." Darcy stopped and blushed. "Oh I wasn't supposed to mention that. Would you excuse me, Dawn, before I spill the beans?"

"Yeah, I was going to lie down for a while anyway."

Darcy whirled. "Are you sick?" Her eyes looked alarmed.

"No. Just a routine nap," she said.

Darcy let out her breath and color returned to her cheeks. "Well, I'll see you at dinner then."

"At dinner," Dawn confirmed, retreating to her room with relief. She set the crystal bear on the table next to her wicker headboard and stared at it. Her thumbprint had smudged its potbelly. Teddy bears were supposed to be soft and cuddly and cute. The crystal one was beautiful, but so lifeless.

Dawn sighed and curled into a ball on her bed. "*. . . spill the beans.*" *Isn't that what Darcy had said? Spill the beans about what?* she wondered.

* * * * *

"You landed on Park Place. I own it and that will cost you $100," Rhonda said, picking up the dice for her turn at the monopoly game.

Dawn counted out the money, listening to the March rain against her bedroom window. Both girls lay stomach down on the floor, stretched out on either side of the board. Bottles of root beer and a bowl of popcorn sat beside them.

"Earth to Dawn. Earth to Dawn. Come in please, Dawn."

Dawn started. "Excuse me?"

"You seem to be in the twilight zone today. What gives?"

"Sorry. You're right. I don't have my mind on the game."

"So what are you thinking about?"

"Darcy. What do you think of her?"

Rhonda sat up and rested backward on her elbows. "Well, she's not ugly."

"Thanks for the news flash. We're having a *special* dinner for her and Rob tonight. Mom's doing a rib roast and baked potatoes. She's even using the good silver and china. Rob bought a centerpiece of red roses, too."

"Sounds romantic."

"Sounds mysterious."

"But isn't this Darcy's last night here? Won't she be going home and taking Rob with her tomorrow?"

Dawn nodded.

"So what's the big deal? Maybe your Mom's just trying to treat her extra nice. Don't you like her?"

Dawn rolled over and planted her elbow on a floor cushion and laid her head against her hand. "It's not that I don't like her. It's just that maybe she's just too perfect for our family. I'll bet she's never even had a hangnail!" Now Dawn felt petty. Darcy

33

couldn't help it because nothing bad had happened to her.

"It doesn't seem fair, does it?" Rhonda's instant understanding surprised Dawn. She looked at Rhonda and wondered why she'd never really thought of her as a good friend before.

"I sound mean, don't I?"

Rhonda shrugged her shoulders. "Some of the girls at school have wondered the same things, Dawn. Why did you get sick? Why not one of us? For that matter, why not me?"

Dawn blushed, thinking about her friends talking about her. She was embarrassed to think that she'd been the topic of conversation. "I—I wish you all wouldn't discuss me..."

"It was never in a bad way," Rhonda added quickly. "Kids feel sorry for you, that's all. And you can't help wondering why it had to happen at all."

The two sat in silence for a few minutes. "I wish it would all go away for you," Rhonda said.

Dawn smiled. "I wish so, too. But, I don't think it's going to go away."

"What do you think's going to happen?" Rhonda leaned forward. Concern and fear showed in her face.

Dawn waited for a moment. Then she said, "I think I'm going to stay in remission for five years, grow up and make a million dollars selling my story to television networks."

Rhonda grinned. "Maybe Darcy can play your mother."

They both began laughing, rolling around on the floor and scattering the Monopoly game every which way.

The conversation she and Rhonda had kept running through Dawn's head, even at the dinner table that night, which she had to admit looked magnificent. The table was draped with her mother's Irish linen cloth and aglow with tall candles. Rob had dressed in a dark suit and Darcy wore a silk dress and pearl stud earrings and matching strands of pearls. Dawn had dressed up, too, but felt dowdy and drab amid the others.

"I guess you wondered why I asked for tonight to be special, Mom and Dad," Rob finally said, interrupting Dawn's thoughts.

Dawn's heart thudded.

Darcy and Rob exchanged glances. Rob took Darcy's left hand and held it up for all of them to see. A diamond glittered off her third finger. "I've asked Darcy to marry me. And she said, yes."

Five

FOR a moment no one spoke. Then everybody spoke at once. There was a round of hugs and a babble of questions. *Married!* Dawn could scarcely absorb it. Rob—her big brother, her only brother—was getting married.

"What do you think, Squirt?"

"I—I think it's great!" Deep down, she meant it. All her funny feelings about Darcy evaporated. "That means I'll be an aunt."

"Whoa, slow down." Mrs. Rochelle said. "Let's get them married first."

Dawn blushed furiously. What a stupid thing to say! she thought to herself.

"Have you set a date?" her father asked.

"This summer."

"August," Darcy added.

Rob said, "We want to go back to college in the fall as husband and wife. We've already begun to check on apartments in East Lansing."

"It isn't easy supporting a wife and finishing your degree," Mr. Rochelle cautioned.

"I'll still have my scholarship plus my part-time job at the men's wear store."

August! Dawn thought. Why that was only five months away.

"Dawn," Darcy said, looking uncomfortable. "If you're feeling up to it . . . that is, if you can handle it . . . ." Darcy stopped and swallowed hard. "Would you like to be a bridesmaid?"

"I—I don't know . . ." Dawn mumbled. *Darcy doesn't really want me to be in her wedding,* Dawn thought. *She just feels sorry for me.*

"How many brothers have you got who are getting married?" Rob teased. "We want you in the wedding, don't we, honey?" He slipped his arm around Darcy's shoulder.

"Of course we do."

"Well, we'll see how I'm doing in August." She hadn't wanted to use her leukemia as an excuse, but it seemed the only logical way to stop Rob from making Darcy do something she didn't want to do.

"Of course," Rob agreed, his eyes looking softly at Dawn.

The table began buzzing again with plans, and the awkward moment passed. But Dawn knew she couldn't forget how uncomfortable Darcy looked when she asked Dawn to be in her wedding. Perfect girls with perfect smiles had perfect weddings. They didn't have bridesmaids whose hair might fall out from chemotherapy or who might get sick and embarrass the bride.

That night, she wrote in her diary:

> *Rob asked if I'd mind having him hanging around Columbus this summer so Darcy and he can make wedding plans. He hasn't lived at home for two years, so it'll be fun having him here again. By the time I get back from camp, there'll only be six weeks left before the big day. I'm still trying to think of a way to get out of being in the actual wedding. I could tell by the look on Darcy's face that she would rather me not be in the ceremony.*

She reread the words and almost scratched them out because they sounded petty. But that's how she felt. If she died, maybe she'd request to have her diary buried with her. It was a morbid idea, but she chuckled in spite of it.

* * * * *

Dawn walked down the silent, empty halls of her school building. The click of her heels on the cement corridors was the only sound. It was the last day of school. The moment the bell had rung, the halls had been filled with rushing, shouting kids, tossing papers and tattered notebooks into garbage cans.

Now, almost an hour later, the rooms were deserted, and the halls were vacant. Why had she stayed? She had told Rhonda that she needed to clean out her locker and that she'd see her later.

"Are you sure?" Rhonda had asked. "I don't mind helping you."

"I need to see Mr. Blake about my Algebra exam, too. I was at the clinic the day of the test and I had some questions." The excuse had sounded lame. After all, she'd passed the test and she knew it.

"Okay. We'll save you a seat at the Pizza Palace." Rhonda had scurried off with Jill and Kathy.

For some reason, she wanted to be alone inside the school where she'd spent her last two years. She *did* have to clean out her locker. But it was more than that. She knew in her heart that she wanted to say good-bye.

"Next year, ninth grade," she said into the empty hallway. Would she be around to return in September? On one locker, someone had scribbled "Mark loves Pamela." Dawn rubbed her thumb over the letters and watched them smear.

Dawn sighed and spun the combination lock on her locker. She looked inside and wrinkled her nose. So that's where she'd left her other pair of sneakers.

"Hi, Dawn." The unexpected male voice startled her. She whirled around and stared straight into the brown eyes of Jake Macka. Her knees went weak.

"Sorry, I didn't mean to scare you. I thought I was the last one here."

"No. I just couldn't bear to leave!" She draped her body dramatically against the lockers.

He grinned and her heart did flip-flops. "It's funny knowing I won't be coming back here next year."

"Yeah. Adams Junior High won't be the same without you." *Stupid comment, Rochelle,* she told herself. *Why not throw yourself at his feet?*

"The real question is: Is Cincinnati ready for Jake Macka?"

A knot settled in her stomach. "Don't you

want to move? It might be sort of fun."

Jake gripped the top of her locker door and glanced inside. "Moving isn't fun. But we do it every time my dad gets a job promotion. What died in there?"

She giggled. "Sneakers and an apple core."

He plucked out the shriveled brown core and heaved it down the hall. "That thing's a health hazard."

Their gazes tripped over one another. "Well, I hope you have a good time in your new school." *Why do I always say such dumb things?*

"Dawn, I—uh, I've been wanting to ask you. Are you all right? I mean . . . healthwise?"

She shrugged. "The doctors say my tests look perfect. That is, perfect for a sick person." Jake averted his eyes. Dawn felt her palms grow clammy. Why couldn't she say anything right today?

"I—uh—I'm glad your hair's growing long again."

She touched it, wishing it were longer. "Me too. It takes such a long time to grow."

"I remember when you used to sit in front of me in English last year—before you got sick. I used to stare straight at the back of your hair. It always looked so soft." Jake's voice dropped and she had to lean forward to catch his next

41

words. "I sometimes wanted to touch it to see if it was as soft as it looked."

Dawn thought her heart would hammer through her chest. Her mouth went dry. "You can touch it now. I mean, since you're moving and all and I'll never see you again. I don't mind if you touch it."

Jake's hand rose and he caught the ends of her hair in the tips of his fingers. "I was right. It is soft."

His eyes were a deep shade of chocolate and she wanted to touch his face. He lowered his hand, brushing her shoulder. "Thank you." He took a step backward. "I hope you never get sick again. I hope your hair grows all the way down to your waist. Good-bye, Dawn Rochelle."

Her tongue stuck to the roof of her mouth. All she could do was watch him walk hurriedly down the hall. *Good-bye. Good-bye, school. Good-bye, Jake. Good-bye, Sandy.* Why did it seem like she was always saying good-bye?

Dawn snatched her sneakers, raked old papers onto the floor, and rushed toward the outside door of the huge, empty school building. She never looked back.

Six

"**D**AWN! Dawn Rochelle! Over here."
Dawn scanned the crowded room and
the scores of campers for the person who had
called out her name. She almost tripped over
the duffle bag of the girl next to her and
wished that all the parents would leave and let
the kids settle into the camp for the next two
weeks on their own.

"Hey, Dawn. How are you?" Mike
McConnell, the boy she'd met the previous
summer who'd lost half his leg to bone cancer,
hobbled over to her on crutches. "I thought
that was you."

Dawn hugged Mike impulsively. Then she
stepped back self-consciously. "Hey yourself.
Why the crutches? Where's your prosthesis?"

"Got a sore spot, so Dr. Ben told me to
leave it off for a few days." The mention of the
camp director's name caused Dawn to giggle

inwardly. Dr. Ben had always been able to act like one of the kids and yet maintain his authority at the same time. Mike added, "You look super. Let's get out of this crowd and walk down by the lake."

They wove their way through the clusters of people and their luggage. In a few minutes they were walking along the familiar leafy trails toward the blue lake that rested in the center of the camp complex. The sounds of activity soon faded into the sounds of the surrounding woods.

"I was hoping someone would be here that I knew," Mike said.

"Didn't Greg come?" Dawn's heart skipped a beat. Had something happened to Greg? They hadn't written since Christmas. Was he all right?

"He got a swimming scholarship at UCLA and went out in June to begin training. Yeah, I'd say old Greg is sitting on top of the world."

"Then he must be—cured." She said the word slowly, almost enviously.

"Let's just say that he beat the odds."

"Too bad Sandy didn't."

"Yeah. Thanks for writing and telling me. It depressed me, but I'm glad you let me know."

The buzz of insects hummed in the air as they reached the edge of the lake. The water lapped at the shoreline. "The lake's down," Dawn said.

"It's been a dry summer," Mike said. Then there was silence for awhile. Mike broke it with, "Going to the campfire tonight?"

Dawn nodded, hugging her arms. "I think that's why I came this year. Sandy sent me her matchbox full of ashes and I felt I needed to return them to the bonfire. Do you know what I mean?"

"Sure. It's like some kind of unfinished business."

"Mike—" she paused. "If things go sour for me—they're fine, honest—but just in case— would you bring back my bonfire ashes next year?"

"Hey." He poked her arm playfully. "You'll be here."

"I know. But just in case . . ."

Mike prodded a stone with the tip of his crutch. "Of course I will. But I expect to see you here next summer. Besides who else can I count on to help me pull another trick on Dr. Ben?"

She smiled sheepishly, relieved to have the conversation turn to a lighter subject. "Yeah, who else would be crazy enough to try to outsmart Dr. Ben two years in a row?"

Her gaze met Mike's and they both grinned

devilish smiles. "Got any wild ideas?" Mike asked.

"I might. Come on. Walk me back to my cabin and we'll think up a way to get him like we did last year with the water balloons."

"It's going to be a hard act to follow," Mike sighed.

"We're up to it. After all, what are friends for?"

Mike started up the trail in step with Dawn. "Right. What else are friends for if not to get into trouble together?"

They returned to their respective cabins, devising pranks and schemes, the soft cocoon of summer seemingly turning back the hands of time.

* * * * *

The bonfire ritual that night was just as Dawn remembered it. The sun set in a fiery ball over the lake. Clusters of campers settled expectantly on logs facing an enormous pyramid of twigs and sticks. Dawn sat next to Mike, feeling the warmth of his shoulder brushing hers. Whispers from other kids buzzed in the gathering darkness, then dwindled as they all watched a canoe slip through the dark waters of the lake toward the shoreline and the wooden pyre.

Two people, dressed as Indians, complete with moccasins and feathers, guided the boat onto the shore and climbed out. They walked silently up to the bonfire. When Dr. Ben, dressed in shorts, a T-shirt, and his familiar baseball hat that said "Top Dog" stood, Dawn felt a warmth for the man who watched over his charges every year. He said solemnly, "The Indians were the first to see this land, the first to travel across this lake, the first to hunt and fish this area. We pay tribute to them and their spirit of harmony with nature."

One Indian lit a torch and held it high into the star-studded sky. "Each year, our ritual is the same," Dr. Ben told the campers. "We light the bonfire, gather 'round, roast marshmallows, and watch the fire burn low. Once the embers cool, each of you will gather some of the ashes in a box, take them home with you, and guard them until next year.

"When you return next summer, bring them and toss them onto that bonfire. In this way, each of us comes back to this place, bringing some of the past, taking some of the future. Will you who have ashes from last year please come forward?" Dawn's heart thudded as she stood, clutching both hers and Sandy's boxes of old ashes in her fist. She felt Mike's reassuring pat on her back as she stepped forward to join a line of other kids.

One by one, the group filed forward, dumping their boxes onto the pyramid of sticks. This is for "Tracy McElroy, who died last February," one girl said as she emptied her boxes. "This is for Martin Clark, who's in the hospital right now," a boy said, following the same routine. Dawn shuffled forward, staring into the tangle of wood. It was her turn. She pulled open the boxes and shook out their contents. "This is for Sandy Chandler who—" she heard her voice catch. "—who went home to God last October." The ashes fluttered onto the pile.

She stepped back and watched as the others went through the line. Every now and again, she'd recognize a name or remember a face. Once the procession was complete, the Indian with the lighted torch advanced and touched his burning flame to the base of the wooden pyramid. The fire caught and soon the rubble of wood burned brightly, crackling and snapping in the summer light. Dawn felt the heat and watched as the flames licked against the canopy of black sky.

Whoops and shouts broke out. The Indians retreated and marshmallows appeared. Dawn tried hard, but she couldn't bring herself to join in the fun. She felt cut off from the others.

All she wanted to do was stare at the golden flames. Mike leaned over her, balancing on one crutch. "Could you give me a hand with this marshmallow? It's got a mind of its own."

Dawn focused on the gooey blackened glob attached to the end of a coat hanger. She shook off her mood. "I don't think you can salvage that one, Mike. Here, let me show you what real talent can accomplish with one of those things." She grabbed the hanger and put a fluffy marshmallow on it. Then she stretched it over the yellow fire, browning it to perfection. "Here," she pulled it off the wire and popped it into his open mouth.

"Scrumptious," Mike declared. He draped his arm over her shoulder and squeezed the base of her neck. "Are you all right?"

"I'm all right."

Firelight glanced off the side of his face as she looked up at him. His eyes reflected concern in the dancing flames. "Can I roast you another one?" she asked.

"Absolutely. What are friends for?"

She smiled and echoed, "What are friends for?"

Seven

"**WHAT'RE** you reading?" Mike asked Dawn, two days later in the camp's giant mess hall. He slid his crutches onto the floor and sat down beside her.

"A letter from my brother, Rob," she answered, glancing up from the page.

"Is that the one you told me about who's getting married?"

"Yes. I'm glad I'm at camp. He says that being around Darcy and our mother is like living in a circus. Darcy's coming to stay for a few days after I get home from camp to make more plans." Dawn rolled her eyes. "Rob says I should elope when it's my turn to get married."

Mike chuckled. "I've got two sisters, but they're five and nine. So I guess we don't have to think about weddings for a while."

"What about you? Or are you going to just

date forever?"

A strange look flitted across his face. He hunkered down and shrugged his broad shoulders. "Not too many girls are hot to go out with a one-legged guy."

Dawn could have bitten her tongue. What a stupid thing to say to him. She'd known he was sensitive about his leg from the previous summer when he wouldn't go swimming. She remembered how Sandy had accepted him, and made him feel accepted by others, too. And Dawn certainly understood how it was to be "different." No guy in her school seemed interested in her as a girlfriend. Jake had been nice to her, but he'd never asked her for a real date. "I felt the same way when I was bald and ugly from chemotherapy. I shouldn't have asked. Sorry."

"No big deal. So have you come up with a plan to get Dr. Ben?" He changed the subject.

"I'm formulating one."

"I'm all ears. When do we strike?"

"After skit night next week. Right before we all have to go home. He'll be so busy concentrating on skit night, he'll have his guard down." She knew that each cabin was secretively planning entertainment skits for trophies and prizes. "What are you guys doing anyway?"

Mike grinned impishly. "It's a secret. But we plan to steal the show."

"Don't count on it. Our cabin is onto something really hot."

Mike waved his hand in dismissal. "You don't stand a chance."

"We'll see about that," Dawn huffed, then tugged on a hank of Mike's hair. "Come on. It's time for arts and crafts."

Mike made a face. "Where can we hide to escape?"

Dr. Ben bustled into the mess hall. "Ah, there you two are. Just in time to help me with crafts for the seven- and eight-year-olds."

Mike groaned and Dawn slouched. Too late. "You two owe me," Dr. Ben said with a wag of his finger. "Don't think I've forgotten last year. I'm glad you're taking it easy on me this year and acting like adults." He smiled.

Dawn put on an innocent expression and looked at Dr. Ben's blue eyes. "Why Dr. Ben . . . we've matured since last summer. We're too old for silly kid pranks. Aren't we, Mike?"

"Much too old."

Dr. Ben cocked his head to one side. "Why don't I believe you?"

Dawn leapt to her feet and Mike struggled up beside her, leaning on his crutch. "I'm putting my prosthesis on tomorrow, and then who knows? Maybe I'll turn into a kid again."

"Is that a warning, McConnell?" Dr. Ben's eyes twinkled.

"Naw. Like Dawn said, we're too old for pranks." They followed the camp director outside. The sunshine was warm and the air smelled fresh and clean. Dawn breathed in and felt a kind of contentment.

* * * * *

"Sh—Sh!" Dawn commanded, crouching behind a long table in the darkened mess hall kitchen. "Mike," she whispered, "turn on the flashlight, but keep the beam low to the floor."

Mike, crouching behind her, snapped the flashlight's button and a narrow stream of light cut through the darkness. "Why do we have to sneak in here for eggs and flour four nights in a row?"

Dawn leaned against the smooth door of the giant refrigerator. "Because if we take too much at once, someone will notice. This way, if we only take a little bit at a time, then we'll have all the supplies we need to get Dr. Ben and no one will be the wiser. Understand?"

Mike grumbled, "You still haven't told me what we're doing to him yet."

"All in good time."

A noise startled them, and they both hugged the floor, hearing footsteps approaching. Mike quickly turned off the flashlight, tugged Dawn's arm, and motioned toward a walk-in pantry door. They crawled inside just as the kitchen light flooded the room. Pressed into the hard pantry shelves, Dawn held her breath. If they were caught, her plan would be ruined. Not to mention her pride. She heard the refrigerator door open and the sound of glass bottles knocking lightly together. *It's only someone after a midnight snack,* she told herself. Within minutes, she heard the door close, saw the light blink off, and heard the sound of the outside door bang shut.

"Whew! That was close." Mike admitted.

"Come on. Let's hurry." Dawn slinked to the refrigerator. She took two eggs and settled them carefully into two pockets in her shirt. She now owned six eggs and two cups of flour. It was all hidden in her suitcase under her bunk in her cabin. She patted her prizes and whispered, "Let's go. Thursday night, during the skit entertainment, we bake our cake."

"What *are* you planning, Dawn Rochelle?"

"You'll see," she replied confidently. "All I can say is that this will be a cake Dr. Ben will remember a long time." Together, they slouched and scurried outside into the night, back to their respective cabins.

* * * * *

The day before skit night, ten-year-old Jennifer Hayes got very ill. Dr. Ben and two of the nurses stayed up with her most of the night, but early the next morning an ambulance had to come for her. The incident left the campers shaken, their spirits dampened. And Dawn felt angry. Why did reality always have a way of rearing its ugly head? They all had cancer. There was no forgetting.

"All right, people! Let's settle down and get this show underway!" Dr. Ben shouted after blowing his whistle. "That's better," he said as excited chatter died down to whispers.

Dr. Ben stood at the front of the room on a makeshift stage, with a blanket for a curtain. "Now, when I call your cabin's name, come up front and get ready behind the curtain. Props and things have been stashed in the kitchen area, so you'll all have five minutes between skits to change. As you know, the staff will act as judges. The winning skit will be awarded a trophy that will go in our permanent trophy case."

"We'll judge on originality and presentation. In the case of a tie," he lowered his glasses and swept his gaze over the audience, "I will act as tie-breaker." Boos and hisses followed his announcement. "No need to get hostile," he shouted. "I'm both fair and perfect." More boos and hisses came from the crowd.

Dawn wiggled on the hard bench. She had more than her cabin's skit on her mind. Her eyes looked for Mike across the crowded room. Their eyes met and he winked. She carefully raised her head to see the paper sack secured above the stage in the rafters. The low light level made it almost invisible. Propped behind the doorway to the kitchen was a broom that Mike had set casually against the wall. With all the activity, it was hard to see the upside down nail protruding from its end. Part one of their plan was in motion.

One by one the cabins went forward to perform. Dawn's cabin—Red Fox—performed their skit dressed as doctors and nurses. Dawn played a receptionist who was hard of hearing and who kept getting the doctor's instructions wrong. The skit went very well. When it was over and they took their bows, Dawn carefully placed two eggs on the chair she knew was Dr. Ben's.

But as funny as their skit had been, it was

Mike's cabin who took the prize. As the curtain parted for the six boys from Hawk Cabin, the audience gasped. There the boys stood, dressed as girls, complete to eye makeup, bright red lipstick, and brilliant pink cheeks. Curly wigs were on their heads and earrings dangled from their ears. And Mike was wearing one of *her* nightgowns! How had he gotten hold of it without her knowing? Across the chest, where he'd placed two bulging balloons, was printed *Kiss Me, You Fool.* Dawn felt her face grow red, but she was laughing too hard to really be embarrassed.

All the boys paraded and danced in their feminine clothes, mouthing the words to a recorded love song by a top female rock singer. Whistles and catcalls came from the audience. Following their performance, the group took three curtain calls.

"Not bad!" Dr. Ben shouted. "Especially the one in the middle!" he said, indicating Mike.

When it came time to present the trophy, it was no contest. Hawk Cabin won! As Mike accepted the trophy, Dawn casually joined him on stage, reaching behind the door for the broom as she went.

"Thanks, Dr. Ben," Mike beamed, holding out his hand.

Dr. Ben shook it and the raw egg concealed in Mike's palm cracked in the camp director's hand. "What the . . !" he shouted. Dawn nudged him backward in his chair. *Splat.* His backside crushed two more eggs. "Oh no!" He shot out of his chair and another two eggs emerged from Dawn's hands to find the top of his head. The goo from the eggs slithered down his hair, over his glasses, and onto his shoulders. "Help!" he cried. Dawn stepped aside and thrust the broom handle straight up. The protruding nail sliced open the paper bag in the rafters and a shower of white flour descended onto the stunned man.

"Gotcha!" Mike shouted. Then he and Dawn bowed on either side of good old Dr. Ben who resembled a sticky, overgrown polar bear. They clasped hands and walked calmly off the stage into the wildly cheering audience.

Eight

"**C**OME on sleepy head. Are you planning to sleep away the day? It's almost 10 A.M." Dawn's mother announced, pulling up the window shade and letting the morning sunlight pour into Dawn's bedroom.

Dawn groaned and buried her face in her pillow. "It's summer vacation."

"You've been sleeping in ever since you got home from camp. Darcy's coming tonight with our wedding invitations. You are going to help me address them, aren't you?"

Dawn sensed her mother standing beside her bed so she peeked through one eye from beneath the pillow. *The wedding invitations. Darcy's visit. Fittings for her bridesmaid dress.* No, she didn't want to get up. She had no energy for these endless projects.

Mrs. Rochelle lifted the pillow off Dawn's face. "Are you feeling all right? Ever since camp and your clinic visit on Monday, you've seemed extra tired."

"Oh, good grief, Mom! Can't a person sleep in if she wants to? Don't make a big deal out of it. I feel just fine." Dawn tossed off her covers and swung to a sitting position. She felt light-headed but she didn't want her mother to know.

"Well, if you say so. Get dressed and come downstairs. Rhonda's called twice. She wants you to go to the mall with her. I'll take you and her mother will pick up. Want to go?"

Dawn felt renewed fatigue just thinking about an excursion to the mall. "Sure. That'll be fun. I'll be down in a few minutes." Her mother left and Dawn flopped backward onto her bed and stretched. What was wrong? Why did she feel so tired? She missed camp and the activity—and the people.

Before she'd left, Mike had walked with her to the lake. He'd asked her, "We had a good time, didn't we?"

She said, "I'll never forget skit night. You were beautiful. You looked better in my nightgown than I do."

"All true. I don't think Dr. Ben will forget it either. We sure got him good. How'll we ever top it next year?"

"We'll think of something."

"Would you—" Mike started. "Would you like to write during the year?"

He continued, "I know I'm not like Greg . . ." Her mind added, *or Jake.* ". . . but I'd like to hear from you. You know, keep in touch."

Dawn smiled up at him and nodded. "Of course, I'd like to write." Then they'd walked back to the main complex and later each of them returned to their cities and homes. Now, a week later, she still hadn't written Mike. "If only I wasn't so tired all the time," she said aloud to her shelves of teddy bears. The menagerie grinned down at her, but didn't answer.

She went downstairs and joined Rob in the kitchen where he was wolfing down a heaping platter of waffles. "Hi, Squirt. Want some?" He'd taken a summer job in a grocery warehouse and often worked the night shift for double pay. His already muscular arms bulged with even more definition. He poured a thick river of syrup and she watched it ooze over the sides of the stack. "They're delicious."

She wrinkled her nose. A queasy feeling gripped her stomach. "No thanks. Cereal's fine for me, Mom."

Mrs. Rochelle set a box of corn flakes in front of Dawn, along with a bowl and a carton of milk. "Mom, I'm going to get some sleep,"

Rob said. "Wake me up by three o'clock, so I can get the cobwebs out of my brain. Darcy should be here by dinner time. I told my boss I'd work a double shift this weekend if I could take tonight and tomorrow off."

Once Rob had shuffled off to bed, Dawn finished her breakfast, determined to try to feel energetic. She called Rhonda, set the plans for the day and by the time they arrived at the mall, she felt more perky.

"What do you think of this?" Rhonda asked, holding up a bright aqua bathing suit in the swim wear department of the mall's largest and most fashionable store.

"The color's super on you. I wish I had a tan like yours."

"So come to the pool with me tomorrow afternoon. I'm taking lunch and spending the entire afternoon. Two hours toasting the front. Two hours toasting the back. And time out to swim and flirt with David Casper. He's a lifeguard this summer you know."

"Oh, I can't. Mom's got me locked into wedding plans. Darcy's coming."

Rhonda wrinkled her nose. "Too bad." She nudged Dawn's arm. "Hey, is that Kim and Cindy over there?" Rhonda waved frantically at two girls from the cheerleading squad who were in the next department. Soon the group was a foursome. For Dawn, it was more of a threesome. She felt left out, like a kid looking through a store window. The other girls didn't understand her the way Rhonda did. And Rhonda became so engrossed with the others that she hardly remembered Dawn was with her.

Dawn hung around on the fringes but was grateful when Rhonda's mom showed and took them home. She was more tired than ever as she dragged up the steps of her front porch. She reached for the door's handle, but her mother flung the door wide and pulled her inside. "Oh, honey. I'm so glad you're home." Worry lines creased her forehead.

"What's wrong, Mom?"

"Dr. Sinclair called. He wants us to meet him at the hospital this afternoon."

Dawn's heart pounded and dizziness descended. "Why?"

"He wouldn't say on the phone. But he wants all of us to be there for the consultation."

"Dad and Rob, too?" Even to her own ears, Dawn's voice sounded small and scared.

"Yes. All of us. The whole family. We're to meet him at five in his office at Children's Hospital."

* * * * *

63

The hospital was a giant brick building. Steam spiraled skyward from the kitchen area. Dawn studied the front of the structure as she approached the entrance. She remembered the first time she'd come here—the smells, the faces, the sense of pulsating life that throbbed from the very walls. Even though it was a hot afternoon, Dawn felt cold and clammy. She didn't want to go inside and she didn't want to meet with the doctor.

An air-conditioned breeze swept over her skin as she followed her parents and brother through sliding glass doors and into the elevator. Dr. Sinclair's office was on the tenth floor. For Dawn, the short elevator ride seemed to take forever.

When they finally arrived, Dr. Sinclair took them to a conference room where another man waited. "This is Dr. Singh," Dr. Sinclair said to all of the Rochelles, but to Dawn in particular.

After a round of introductions, they sat and faced each other across a wide oak table—the Rochelles on one side, the doctors on the other.

The faint odor of lemon wax made her nauseous. She told herself that it wasn't the smell, but the tension she was feeling. Her father cleared his throat, and Dr. Sinclair opened a thick manila file on the table in front of him. "Thank you for coming on such short notice."

"We assume it's about Dawn," Dawn's father said.

"Yes." Dr. Sinclair lifted a paper out of the file. "These are the results of her latest bone marrow aspiration tests. What they say is that Dawn's marrow is producing more immature cells than on her previous tests."

"Do you mean I failed my test?" she asked.

A kind, soft smile flipped the corner of the blond-haired doctor's mustached mouth. "Not exactly. What they tell us is that you may be headed for a relapse, a resurgence of your leukemia."

Nine

FOR a moment no one spoke. Dawn felt a buzzing sensation inside her head and listened to the hum of the air conditioning.

Out of remission. Relapse. My cancer's back. She sagged slightly in the chair, feeling almost relieved. Hadn't she been expecting this news for months now? At least now the waiting was over.

"What exactly does that mean?" Rob's voice broke the tension in the room.

"It means that conventional therapy is failing."

"And just what is modern medicine going to do to help my sister now that your conventional therapy is failing?" Rob said angrily. His face looked pinched and white.

Dawn reached over and patted his hand.

Rob flinched and directed his question to the two doctors. "I asked you, what are you hot-shot medical whiz brains going to do about it?"

Dr. Sinclair shuffled the papers in his hands. "That's why I've had Dr. Singh join us. He's the head of the bone marrow transplant unit here at Children's Hospital. Based on what we know about Dawn's case, he feels that she is a candidate for a transplant operation."

"Explain, please," Mrs. Rochelle broke in.

Dr. Singh cleared his throat. "As you may remember, when Dawn was first diagnosed, we extracted bone marrow from each of you and cross-matched it for compatibility. More and more we're successfully reversing the course of leukemia by transplanting healthy, cancer-free bone marrow into victims. There are drawbacks, but if the procedure works, the new bone marrow begins to take over blood cell production and cures the cancer victim."

"So why haven't you done this for Dawn before now?"

Dr. Singh's voice was soft with only a hint of an accent. "The procedure is not without risks."

"What risks?" Dawn's question startled herself. Had she spoken aloud?

Dr. Singh turned toward her. "I will be most honest with you Dawn, because this is truly the most important decision of your life.

Unfortunately, we do not have a genetic match with your bone marrow. Your brother Rob comes the closest."

Rob interjected, "She can have all my bone marrow she needs."

"That is not the problem. Compatibility is the secret of successful transplants. The closer alike her marrow is to yours the better the chances of her body accepting the transplant." Dr. Singh leaned over the table, closer to Dawn. "Do you understand about the human body's defense mechanism? Do you know what biological rejection is?"

"I've studied it some in science class. Everybody has special cells to fight germs. It's like a little army inside us that helps keep us well."

"Excellent, Dawn. That is correct. Your body does not understand or accept any genetic code but your own. If we transplant Rob's bone marrow into you, your body will attack it as if it were germs."

"Then how can you do such a transplant?" Rob asked.

"We prepare Dawn's body with massive doses of immune suppressant drugs. They will hold down her resistance to your marrow, Rob. Hopefully, they will hold it down so that your marrow will start growing and producing healthy blood cells."

"So what are the other risks?"

"By suppressing her immune mechanism, she is also susceptible to any germ or virus that comes along. Even a common cold can be deadly."

Dawn felt removed from the conversation, as if they were discussing a character on a television show instead of her. "How long before you know if Rob's bone marrow is working inside me?" Dawn asked.

"The entire process will take about six weeks. First you will check into the hospital and undergo testing. If all things point to success, you will be placed into isolation and a sterile room and the immune suppressant drugs will begin. After they do their job, Rob will have an operation and a portion of his bone marrow removed. We will give it to you much as you receive your chemotherapy. It will drip slowly into your body over a four- or five-hour period. You will be awake the whole time. If all goes well, you will leave the hospital a few weeks later. Assuming there are no complications," he added. "Like secondary infections. Or rejection in spite of the drugs."

Silence again filled the room. Dawn wondered briefly if the two doctors realized that there was a moth flapping against the plate glass window behind them. She studied the insect as it flailed and beat its wings on the clear glass, desperate to touch the sun outside. *Poor moth . . .*

"This is not a decision for you to make right now, Dawn," Dr. Sinclair said, breaking the heavy silence. "Go home and think about it. Discuss it. But don't take too long. We'll need to proceed as soon as possible if you decide in favor of the procedure."

"The odds," Rob said. "What are the odds of the transplant succeeding?"

The two doctors exchanged quick glances. "Without it, Dawn has a twenty percent chance of survival. With it, fifty-fifty."

* * * * *

Dawn moved dinner around on her plate with her fork. She had no appetite, in spite of her mother's best efforts at fried chicken and the bright, forced smiles of her family and Darcy.

"So what did you think of the invitations?" Darcy asked.

"They're very nice," Mrs. Rochelle said. "Don't you think so Dawn?"

Dawn recalled scrolled black letters on stiff ivory paper:

> Mr. and Mrs. Oliver Collins and Mr.
> and Mrs. Peter Rochelle request the
> honor of your presence at the
> marriage of their children Darcy
> Lynn and Robert Clark . . .

She shrugged. "Yes, the invitations are very nice."

"If you have your operation . . . will it be after the wedding?"

Dawn gaped at Darcy, blinked and shook her head, as if she hadn't heard her correctly. How could Darcy ask such a thing? Was she afraid Dawn would mess up her perfect row of bridesmaids by being in the hospital during the ceremony? Dawn dropped her fork and rose from the table. "Excuse me. I'm not hungry."

She left the kitchen hurriedly, hearing Rob's harsh words as she bounded up the stairs to her room. "Good grief, Darcy! How could you ask such a dumb thing? Don't you understand what Dawn's going through?"

It was quiet and dark in her room. What was she going to do? What? She thought about going back into the hospital. She remembered the needles, the tubes, the pills . . . . She shuddered, thinking of the antiseptic rooms and endless hallways. But this time there was an additional worry. Would she ever come out

71

again? Once inside, would she ever walk out into the sunshine? Would she really be cured?

Dawn ambled to the window and watched filmy clouds flit across the face of the full moon. How many moons were left for her? She absently picked Mr. Ruggers off the shelf and twirled him by his frayed ears. She brought him to her chest and hugged his fat, overstuffed body. His black plastic nose was loose. He'd probably lose it soon. "Poor, Mr. Ruggers," she said aloud. "No nose, no toes, no woes." The bear offered a lopsided smile.

Dawn sighed. *"It's your decision,"* the doctors had told her. *"Tell us what you want to do, sweetheart,"* her parents had said. *"Will your operation be after the wedding?"* Darcy had asked. Why didn't anyone understand that the decision was too big for her? Too hard? How could she decide when one direction meant—dying?

From below her window, Dawn heard angry voices. Rob and Darcy stood by the oak tree in the middle of the back yard.

"But Rob," Dawn heard Darcy's voice say. "It's my *wedding* day! I only plan to be married once in my life. Stop treating me like I'm the Wicked Witch of the West because I want it to be perfect."

"Then stop acting like postponing it is the end of the world."

"But the invitations . . . "

"She's my sister, Darcy. Don't you understand? She needs me. Only my bone marrow will do. I can't help it if the timing messes up our wedding plans."

Dawn saw Darcy reach out and touch Rob's shoulder. He jerked away. "Don't. Please, Rob. I love you."

Dawn withdrew from her position by the window. It wasn't right to eavesdrop. She stared vacantly up at the moon, all the while running her thumbs over Mr. Ruggers' fur, feeling the bald places, rubbed smooth by years of cuddling. She lay the animal against her cheek and said, "It isn't fair, Mr. Ruggers. It just isn't fair." Her cancer had ruined her life. And now it was ruining her brother's.

Ten

DAWN asked her family not to tell anyone about the suggested bone marrow transplant. She needed time to think, to decide what to do. The next day, she asked Rhonda to meet her at the mall. They met at the mall's entrance, Rhonda breezing in late.

"Sorry, but I couldn't decide what to wear," she told Dawn.

Dawn nodded sympathetically. "Sometimes deciding what to wear can really be a pain."

Rhonda looked at her skeptically. "Well, it's *not* easy deciding, you know. I have lots of new clothes from my babysitting work and I wanted to dress just right."

"I didn't mean to offend. I know some decisions can be tough." How lucky Rhonda was to have nothing more serious to decide than what outfit to wear! "Come to the ladies room and let me show you the new makeup I bought. I thought it would be fun to put it on before we walked around."

Rhonda looked surprised. "I thought you said that your parents wouldn't let you wear a lot of makeup."

"Well I feel like living dangerously," Dawn said with a flip of her hand. "I spent my entire month's allowance at the makeup counter. Aren't you going to help me experiment?"

"Well—uh—sure. But . . . gee Dawn. This doesn't seem like you. Living dangerously and all."

"I'm bored and tired of being sweet little Dawn. Now are you coming or not?"

Rhonda tagged behind as they entered a well-lit public rest room. No one else was there. Dawn opened her large canvas purse and pulled out new boxes of makeup—eye shadows, blusher, mascara, three shades of lipsticks, and two eye-liners. Rhonda's eyes grew round with awe. "Wow. You sure did blow your allowance."

"What the heck. It's only money." Dawn stroked the bright pink blusher over her cheek bones. She lined her eyelids in emerald green and smudged on green shadow. She surveyed her reflection. "What do you think?"

"Not bad. Here, let me use some." Soon, Rhonda's face matched Dawn's. "Boy this is fun! I like the new Dawn."

"Did you think the old one was too much of a goodie-goodie?"

Rhonda flushed. "Of course not. I mean, you can't help being . . . different."

Dawn ignored the remark. "I read that if you powder your lashes first and then put on mascara, they'll look twice as thick."

"I'm game." After a dusting of face powder, both girls layered black mascara on their lashes.

"Great!" Rhonda said.

Dawn held up two shades of lipstick, "Which one for you?"

"Coral." Rhonda put on the one color and Dawn smeared on the hot pink one.

"Let's do our hair, too." Dawn chose to rake hers to one side and nestle a lime green comb to hold it in place behind her ear. "I got some new perfume, too." She spritzed the air and Rhonda sniffed.

"Nice stuff. I'll bet you're flat broke."

"Who cares? I wanted the stuff. After all, you only live once." Dawn squirted the heady, floral aroma behind her ears, on her throat, and on her wrists. She gazed at her mirror image for a studied moment. She didn't look like Dawn anymore. She looked older, more grown up. "I like it, Rhonda. Do you suppose

76

anyone will notice how beautiful we are?"

"Maybe some movie scouts will discover us."

"In Columbus? What would they be filming—'Frankenstein Goes to the Mall'?" Dawn giggled at her own joke.

"Come on," Rhonda chided. "We look great. I bet we could even pass for sixteen."

Dawn puckered her lips. "Sixteen and a beauty queen."

Rhonda squirted on some perfume. Then she said, "Let's get some pizza at Tony's. I'm starved."

"All right, but you'll have to treat because I'm broke."

They headed for the little pizzeria in the mall between two fashion boutiques. Inside, the restaurant was lit by small lamps with red checkered shades. The air smelled of cheese and pizza dough.

"Here's a booth," Rhonda said, sliding across a red vinyl cushion.

Dawn checked out her menu. "I really feel daring. How about anchovies?"

Rhonda wrinkled her nose. "Get serious. Mushrooms and sausage is all I can handle."

They giggled and nibbled on breadsticks as they waited to order. Dawn peered around the room. Couples sat at several tables. She wondered what it would be like to go on a date, a real date with a guy to talk to and hold hands with. Would she think of anything to say? Or would she just sit and stare stupidly at him?

"Don't look now, but those two guys over there are staring at us." Rhonda's excited whisper interrupted Dawn's thoughts.

"Where?"

"Don't turn around, dummy!" Rhonda commanded. "Just act casual."

Dawn flipped her hair off her shoulders and scanned the room. Sure enough, two boys sitting at a nearby table were looking her way.

"They look older than us," Dawn whispered at Rhonda.

"So what? We're sixteen in our new makeup."

Dawn felt her heartbeat increase. "But that was just for fun . . ."

"Oh, my gosh! They're heading this way!" Rhonda squealed under her breath.

From the corner of her eye, Dawn saw two males stop at their booth. A deep voice said, "Hi."

She looked up into the faces of boys she didn't know. "Hi," she mumbled.

"Couldn't help but notice that you two were all alone," the taller of the boys said.

"Thought we'd introduce ourselves. Maybe join you if you're not waiting for someone."

"Sure, that's fine," Rhonda said. "We're all alone."

Dawn shot her friend a murderous glance.

The two boys slid into the booth and Dawn pressed close to the wall. Her heart hammered and her mouth went cotton dry. She took long sips from her water glass.

"I'm Ricky," the boy next to her said. "This is my friend, Todd. We go to Westerville High. How about you?"

"Worthington High," Rhonda lied.

Again, Dawn fixed a killing gaze on her friend.

"What's your name?" Ricky's question was directed at Dawn and she couldn't avoid it.

"Dawn."

"A pretty name for a pretty girl."

"How can you tell? It's dark." Her hands started to shake and she was afraid she'd drop her water glass.

"It's not *that* dark. You don't have to squeeze up against the wall. I won't bite."

The others at the table laughed and Dawn felt her face flush. "I—I'm not . . ."

Across the room, a waitress brought Ricky and Todd's pizza to their empty table. "Over here," Ricky called. "We'll be eating it over here at this table."

The waitress set the pan on the center of the checkered cloth. "Have some?" Ricky asked.

"Ours will be coming soon," Dawn told him, positive that she'd choke to death on anything she tried to eat just then.

"So we'll share." His voice was low. Rhonda was busy talking to Todd and wasn't paying any attention to Dawn. She thought about kicking Rhonda under the table, but she was afraid she'd miss and kick Todd.

Ricky rested his arm casually on the back of the booth. "So, Dawn, tell me about yourself."

She felt his hand ease onto her shoulder.

"There's nothing to tell . . ."

"I bet there is. A good-looking girl like you must have a hundred things to tell."

She thought about Mike. *"Who wants to date a one-legged boy?"* She thought about Greg. He'd kissed her. She thought about Jake. He'd never kissed her. She thought about Rob. He loved Darcy. Who would love Dawn? She turned her face. It was inches from Ricky's.

Suddenly, the thought of Ricky touching her made her skin crawl. Dawn jumped up. "I gotta go."

The others turned startled expressions on

her. She forced past Ricky, almost crawling over his lap.

"Hey wait a minute," Ricky called. But she was already half-running to the ladies room. She darted inside and leaned against the wall, waiting for her breath to catch up with her. She began to shake all over. *What's wrong with me. What's wrong with me?* She felt sick to her stomach but it wasn't because of any chemotherapy.

The face in the mirror glared back at her. Quickly Dawn squirted soap in her palm and rubbed until the makeup smeared and ran. She splashed cold water from the faucet, rubbing and rubbing until all traces of the color were gone. She stared at the clean, scrubbed, damp face, recognizing herself once again. Carefully she cleaned out the sink, drying it with paper towels until no traces remained of her "dangerous living."

In a few minutes, Rhonda would figure out that Dawn wasn't returning and she'd come looking for her. What would she say? Dawn recombed her hair, knowing there was nothing she could say that Rhonda would understand. All at once, she felt childish and stupid and tired and drained. All she wanted to do was to go home.

* * * * *

Dawn hadn't realized that night could last so long. She'd lain awake and watched the hands of her clock radio glow in soft shades of digital green until almost four in the morning. After a few fitful hours of sleep, she went downstairs to the kitchen. Her family sat clustered around the breakfast table.

Dawn stood in the doorway, studying each one silently. Her father was reading the morning paper and sipping black coffee. He looked fresh in his crisp business suit. He adjusted his reading glasses. *When had his hair turned gray at the temples?* Mrs. Rochelle buttered her toast and turned over the section of the paper she was reading. Dawn thought, *She's had that old flowered robe for ages. We should get her a new one . . .* Were those streaks of gray in her almost black hair? Rob was hunched over the sports section, a half-eaten cantaloupe in front of him. *He looks tired. He's working too hard and too long.* Mist filmed over her eyes and a lump swelled inside her throat. She cleared it and three pairs of eyes snapped in her direction.

"Good morning," Dawn's mother said, holding out her hand for Dawn to clasp. "Did you sleep well? How about some toast? Cantaloupe too, if you want it."

Dawn took her mother's hand and squeezed

it. "In a minute." She scanned their faces, as if memorizing every line and pore. "I—I made my decision. I know what I want to do about the transplant." Rob nodded encouragement. "I'm tired of being sick. I want to live! Tell Dr. Singh I'm going for the cure."

Rob beamed her a smile and her parents mouthed their agreement. She told her brother, "I know this will mess up your wedding plans . . ."

He interrupted, "I've already told Darcy that our wedding is on hold. We'll just move it to Christmas. It's no big deal."

Dawn had made up her mind. She'd go to the hospital and have the transplant. She'd take the immune suppressant drugs, she'd endure the endless testing and medicines and treatments. Maybe the transplant would be successful. "Until Christmas," she said. By Christmas it would all be over for her, one way or the other.

Eleven

*A*UGUST 3

I haven't been keeping you real up-to-date, diary, but now that I'm checked into the hospital and settled into my room, I promise to write in you everyday.

Dawn reread her words and laughed at herself. As if her diary *cared* whether she wrote in it everyday. But she was determined to write down as much as possible about her transplant experience.

I checked in at 8:30 this morning. It's different being part of a transplant operation from a regular old sickie on the oncology floor. There's a whole team of people just on my case. I even have my own special nurse, Katie O'Ryan. She has red hair and blue eyes and is really young. I like her a lot. I have my own special room. No roommate. It's full of machines and equipment and squeaky clean. Mom likes that part.

They did a bunch of tests today. On Rob too, since he's my donor. Dr. Singh did a bone marrow biopsy on me because they're going to "harvest" my marrow and freeze it. That way, if I reject Rob's marrow, they can put mine back in me and keep me alive.

"Didn't you like your supper?" The question came from Katie, who breezed into the room with a thermometer and blood pressure cuff. Dawn laid down her pen and wrinkled her nose at the hospital supper tray. "Remember," Katie warned, "nothing by mouth after nine o'clock tonight so we can do your harvesting operation in the morning."

"I'll eat a good lunch afterward," Dawn promised. "How's my brother?"

Dimples showed from the sides of Katie's mouth. "For a big strong football player, he sure is a baby about needles. I thought he was going to faint when I gave him a shot."

"Where'd you give it?"

Katie's blue eyes twinkled, "Right smack in his rump."

Dawn giggled. "Bet it was more than the

85

needle that made him faint." She watched as Katie strapped on the blood pressure cuff and squeezed the black bulb. "Am I gonna feel awful tomorrow?"

"You'll be asleep most of the day. But by this time tomorrow night, you'll be refusing more hospital food." Katie offered a comforting smile.

"I wish it were all over. Tell me again what's going to happen."

"After a few more days of testing, we'll put you into isolation and begin the immune suppressant drugs. A week later, after the drugs do their job, Rob will have his operation to remove his bone marrow which we'll put into you. Then we watch and see if it takes. After that, it's only a matter of time until your release and you go home."

Home. How wonderful that word sounded. Already she missed her bedroom and her shelves of teddy bears. *Grow up,* she instructed herself. Teddy bears and fourteen didn't go together.

That night she prayed that she would go home again. She dreamed about Rob playing football with a long plastic tube hanging from his side. It ran the length of the field, up into the stands where she sat, and attached to her side. In the dream, he went out for a pass. The tubing stretched taunt and the ball fell to the ground, useless, at his feet. Dawn knew it was her fault that he was tied down and his team was losing the game—her fault.

Early the next morning, someone woke her long enough to give her a shot that made her drowsy. She dozed, feeling sensations, hearing voices and noises, until hands lifted her from her bed onto a gurney that rolled her down a hallway. She watched the lights slip by overhead. Doors to an operating room swung open and a doctor in a pale green mask and a green cap leaned over her. She recognized Dr. Singh's brown eyes. "How are you doing, Dawn?"

She tried to speak but couldn't form words. Dr. Singh patted her arm. "The anesthesiologist will give you a few puffs of gas and you will go to sleep. When you wake up, you will be back in your room. You're going to be just fine."

Dawn attempted to nod, but her head lolled to one side. Another masked doctor's face appeared. He smiled and slipped a rubber mask over her nose and mouth. He said, "Breath deeply." She took two deep breaths and drifted off into a gray fog . . . .

Dawn felt sore all over. Every inch of her body hurt. She moaned, and instantly saw her parents and Rob next to her bed. "Hi, Squirt. We thought you were going to sleep all day."

87

"Time?"

"Three o'clock."

A bag of blood hung from a stand next to her bed and dripped into a tube through a needle inserted in her arm. Her eyes looked at it curiously.

"Your red blood count was a little low," Rob explained. "So they're giving you a fresh supply. This place would be a vampire heaven," he joked. His tone turned more serious. "You did real well, Dawn. Dr. Singh tells me that if I do half as well for my operation, he'll put a gold star on my chart."

She wanted to smile. "Kate . . . give . . . shot?"

Rob's face assumed a pained expression. "She used me for a dart board. And enjoyed it, I might add. But I'm tough, I can take it. Go back to sleep and we'll see you in the morning." Obediently, she closed her eyes and slept.

When Dawn awoke again, Katie was taking her blood pressure. "Good morning. How do you feel?"

Dawn groaned. "My hip's sore."

"That's where they removed the marrow," Katie said. "We'll let you rest this morning, but you're scheduled for X-ray and skin testing to check out how your immunity system is working this afternoon."

"There are so many tests . . ."

"They're all necessary, honey." Katie's blue eyes were kind. "Phase two is the immune suppressant drugs and transplant. We want that to be successful. But good news— between phases, you can check out of the hospital for a few hours."

"I can?" Dawn felt a bubble of excitement.

"Your family can take you out for dinner right before you go into isolation."

Anticipation filled her. *Outside the hospital.* It would be like getting out of prison. Then another thought occurred. Didn't they give condemned prisoners a last meal?

* * * * *

Just like Katie had said, Dawn was allowed to check out of the hospital with her family for an evening two days before the transplant operation. Mr. Rochelle took them to the finest restaurant in the city. Silverware gleamed, gold-rimmed china shone, and crystal water goblets reflected sparkles of light from candles set on tables. Waiters were dressed in black tuxedos and one made a fancy Caesar's salad at their table, grinding pepper from a tall pepper mill.

The food tasted delicious and as she glanced

around the table at her parents and brother, Dawn wished she had the words to tell them how much they meant to her. She nibbled on a breast of chicken smothered in some French sauce and longed for the night to last forever. But the world of violin music and fresh flowers and beautiful food would be gone in a few hours. Then she would be locked in a world of sterility and antiseptic walls.

When they returned to the hospital she asked Rob, "Can we sit out here on the wall for a few minutes? The night's so beautiful and it's hard to go back inside. I'm not positive I'll be able to come out again."

He lifted her up on the low brick decorative wall, then boosted himself up next to her. "In six weeks you'll walk straight out that door," he said with determination. "There's a whole team of medical geniuses in there devoted to nothing but your cure."

"I'm scared, Rob."

"Me too. But if anyone can do it, you can."

Dawn took deep breaths and stared straight up at the heavens. "The stars make me feel sort of unimportant. Don't you ever wonder what it would be like to touch them?"

"You're more important than all those stars."

" 'For everything there is a season.' " She

quoted from the page in the Bible she'd found in Sandy's keepsakes. "How much longer is my season, Rob?"

He put his arm around her and pulled her close. "If my bone marrow's any good, you'll have a hundred seasons."

"I'm not afraid of dying. It's just that I don't want to yet."

"Hey, don't talk that way. You're going to make it."

Tomorrow, Dawn thought to herself. Tomorrow she would begin phase two of her treatment. Once started, she would be committed to the transplant and the cure. After tomorrow, there was no turning back.

Twelve

DAWN began her immune suppressant drugs with five large capsules containing 34 smaller pills. In the afternoon, a special team scrubbed down her room to make it sterile. She watched the procedure from the doorway as disinfectants and germ killers were sprayed and rubbed into every corner and across every surface. Once back inside the room, she perched on her hospital bed, waiting, as they replaced the equipment after first passing it under ultra-violet light.

"Kills all the little germs and viruses that insist on hanging around," Katie quipped from behind the green surgical mask covering her mouth.

"Will everyone have to dress like that to visit me?" Dawn asked. Katie's small body seemed lost in the green gown. A cap, gloves and special coverings for her shoes made her look like an escapee from an operating room.

"Absolutely," Katie said. "Gowning out is hard for visitors, but it's important. We don't want any bad old germs hitching a ride into this sterile environment. Outside your door is a sign that says: *ISOLATION*. It means it. But, don't worry. You'll see plenty of people. And your TV set is safe. You can 'see the world' every time you turn it on."

Dawn stuck out her lower lip. "TV and books. What a drag!"

"You're forgetting your exercise bike," Katie pointed to the contraption near a wall that looked like a bicycle without wheels. "You can adjust the tension on the handlebars and you'll feel as if you're pedaling up the sides of mountains. And don't forget all the wonderful food we'll be serving you."

A half-smile lifted the corner of Dawn's mouth. "I'm already feeling a bit sick to my stomach from the drugs. The idea of eating really turns me off." She picked at the bedsheets stretching across her lap, hating to ask the question on her mind. "Will there be any other side effects? Will I lose my hair again?"

Katie puckered her mouth, then nodded. "Yes, honey. You'll lose your hair again."

Tears welled up in Dawn's eyes. She

struggled to fight them down. *I don't want to cry. I don't!* "It's just that it took so long to grow . . . I was hoping I wouldn't lose my hair again."

Katie patted her arm. "Hair grows. And so will your brother's bone marrow once we get it in you. Both will grow together."

What does it matter? Dawn thought. Who cared if she got bloated and bald? School, camp, Mike, and Jake seemed a lifetime away. Dawn curled up into a ball and squeezed her eyes shut to keep the tears inside.

* * * * *

The hours and days passed in a haze for Dawn. They gave her pills and dripped concoctions into her veins that made her sick, then disoriented. She couldn't keep her wits long enough to carry on a conversation on some days. She exercised and watched TV and worked puzzles until the medications made her vision blur. She wanted her family with her, then wanted everybody to leave her alone. She got sick. So sick they had to begin feeding her through tubes because nothing would stay down. She saw her legs and hands swell with retained fluids.

They attached her to machines to measure

her heart rate and did chest X-rays and showed her relaxation exercises to practice whenever she was awake. Finally, they took a sample of her bone marrow and pronounced it "knocked out." The thought was mind-boggling. She was defenseless. She was without any of her inborn genetic ability to fight off germs. "But you're also unable to fight off Rob's bone marrow," Katie reminded her.

The day before the transplant, they moved more sterile equipment into the room. "In case anything happens," Dr. Singh told her. She didn't want to consider what might happen. That night Rob came up to visit. He had already checked into the hospital for his early morning operation to remove his bone marrow.

"You look pale," she chided. "Worried about that shot they're going to give you?"

His eyes crinkled. "They sent a nurse who weighed two hundred pounds and stood six-foot-two to give me my last shot."

"Gee, the male nurses are real gentle with me."

"What male nurse?"

She attempted to giggle. "Is Darcy going to wait with Mom and Dad during your operation?"

Rob's eyes darted around the room. "No. I

told her I'd call when I felt like talking. No use for her to sit around all day since I'll be zonked out most of the time."

Dawn studied him, wishing her mind were sharper. He seemed like he was hiding something but she felt too tired to dwell on it. "Thanks, Rob. Thanks for doing this for me."

"Thanks for letting me do it for you," he said.

"Will you come see me as soon as you can?"

"As soon as they let me." Their gazes locked and when he left, Dawn clutched her sheets feeling overwhelmed with gratitude. She hoped Darcy realized how lucky she was to have someone like Rob in her life.

The next morning, Dawn waited in her room with her mother for the nurses to bring in the marrow, signaling that Rob's operation was over. "It's hard not being able to be in two places at once, isn't it, Mom?"

Mrs. Rochelle shrugged and thumbed absently through a magazine. "Your father's with Rob."

Dawn grew thoughtful, staring up at the ceiling. Her mind was full of memories of her and Rob as kids. "When I was little, Rob and I watched a western movie on TV together. I still remember it. In the story two boys, one white and one an Indian, became 'blood brothers.' They cut their fingers and pressed them together so their blood would mingle. It meant they would forever be friends. Brothers. I asked Rob a bunch of questions about it because I thought it was the neatest idea for sealing friendship that I'd ever seen. I guess this makes him and me more than blood brothers, doesn't it?"

Mrs. Rochelle nodded. "I guess it does."

At 11:30, physicians dressed in operating gowns and masks arrived with a bag of what looked like red jello. "It's 1500 cc's of bone marrow," Katie explained. "45 billion cells." She hooked the bag and its tubing to a metal stand and inserted a needle into one of the tubes protruding from Dawn. Her mother gripped Dawn's hand and they watched as the nurse adjusted the drip. "It'll take almost five hours, so relax. I'll take your vital signs every 15 minutes. If you feel itchy or if I see a rash, it may indicate rejection. But we're only going to think good thoughts."

"How's Rob?"

"Sleeping like a baby. He'll be up and around by tomorrow."

Dawn stared at the bag for long minutes, feeling a lump swell in her throat. *Rob's bone marrow.* For her, it was the gift. She closed her eyes and imagined the red, healthy cells pouring into her body, each prepared to set up a permanent home within her bones.

*　*　*　*　*

The days flowed past Dawn without measurement. Dawn understood life from the perspective of a guinea pig. She was poked and prodded and tested almost around the clock. Electrodes on her chest sent her heartbeat to a monitor. Its incessant beeping kept her from sleeping. She felt hot and dried out. "You have a fever," Dr. Singh told her with a shake of his head. It scared her, because the fever could mean rejection.

They gave her antibiotics and she broke out in a rash. "Allergic," the doctor pronounced. She began to swell and the nurses drained fluid from her tissue. Her chest felt tight and that compounded her fears. They gave her pain medications that made her feel groggy, like she were floating in a sea of taffy. No matter how hard she tried, she couldn't think clearly.

Rob hobbled in, bent over. "Still sore," he apologized. "Yuck! I feel sixty years old. I can barely move, but they say it'll be better in the next few days. How are you doing?"

"Tired . . ." Her mouth felt parched, but at least she could talk. "Your bone marrow's working hard. They said my white count was up to 700."

"It had better work hard."

She watched him turn his head through puffy, swollen eyelids. *Were those tears in his eyes?* She didn't want him to cry for her. "How's Darcy? Think you'll be able to stand at the altar by Christmas time?"

He glanced towards the door. "I'll be fine in a few days. All I want for Christmas is for you to be home. Maybe we'll wrap you up and stuff you under the tree."

"Wrap me in red paper. Green bow . . ." Her mind wandered. "Did you make a touchdown in the game last week?"

"I—I—of course."

"That's good. I want to go home. Help me get out of bed, Rob. I'll get dressed and you can drive me home."

His hands pushed her down. "No, honey. You can't leave."

She heard the beeping of her heart monitor grow faster. "If you unplug that stupid thing, we could go home." Her breath came in rapid gasps. Her hands clutched at the front of his gown. "Please . . . take me home."

From somewhere, she heard Katie's voice. "Lie down, Dawn. Please don't try to get up."

Dawn felt more hands on her. Cool hands.

Hot. Why was she so hot? Why didn't they take off her covers? Turn up the air conditioning? She twisted, hearing snatches of words like, "delirious," "spiking fever," "infection." Who were they discussing? Who was sick? She was getting well. Rob's bone marrow was beginning to function. It was hers now—hers. They couldn't take it away from her.

"I'm giving her another pain shot," she heard Katie say. Numbing waves washed over her. She jerked to escape the mire that sucked her into the bedsheets, but she was held fast, a prisoner of another medication.

Thirteen

*D*EAR *Dawn—also known as "Squirt",*

I'm writing in your diary because you're too sick to write in it yourself. Don't worry, I didn't read any of it, because it's private. But I know you want to keep a journal about your transplant. So I thought I'd help out.

First of all, right now you're really sick with some infection. Actually, there's more than one infection. Some, Dr. Singh can fight with antibiotics. Others, we were hoping my bone marrow would go after. Believe it or not, the old Rob Rochelle cells are starting to kick in and the doctors think that if they can clear up these infections, you'll have an excellent response to the transplant.

Please get well. We're all rooting for you, Sis. Your transplant team is super and they care so much about you. The folks and I hope you know we're at your bedside round the clock. I have the morning shift . . .

Rob stopped writing and stared pensively at his sister's motionless form. He'd been with her since five that morning, refusing to even go out for breakfast. She didn't resemble his sister in any way. Her face was swollen and her other features were misshapen and exaggerated by excess fluid. A fine red rash covered her arms and neck. Her hair had fallen out, but Katie had covered her head with a bright pink scarf. It helped, making her look like a toy store doll with fat rosy cheeks and plump, pouting lips.

Tubes and wires attached to machines stuck out of her body, also swollen by retained fluid. Why couldn't she be well? Why couldn't her doctors find the right combination of drugs and heal her? Hadn't they said that the transplant seemed "optimistically good?" With a frustrated sigh, Rob shut the diary and slid it into Dawn's bedside drawer. The uncomfortably hot mask and gown he wore was made worse by the waiting.

"How's she doing?" Mrs. Rochelle asked the question, entering the room while tying the strings of her mask.

"No change." Rob said.

"Your father's gone to his office. He'll come to the hospital after supper tonight."

"You should get some sleep, Mom. I plan to spend the day here. You know I'll call if there's any change."

"Has she asked for me?"

"She's in and out of consciousness. Doesn't make much sense when she's awake. I wish I could do more for her. She keeps asking if you need her for the fitting of her bridesmaid dress."

"She doesn't know about you and Darcy yet?"

Rob flashed his mother a warning glance. "No. And don't say anything about it in this room. You know what Dr. Singh said about Dawn being able to hear us. Just because she can't respond doesn't mean she doesn't know what's going on." The doctor had told them that noise was the one thing that even comatose patients responded to. Often, Dr. Singh would talk very loudly to Dawn, or clap his hands next to her ear. So far, she always responded with a twitch or a moan. He considered it a good sign.

Mrs. Rochelle reached out and touched Rob's arm. "I'll go home in a while. Let me stay with her for right now. Take a drive and get out in the sunshine. Come back around lunch time."

Grateful for his mother's offer, Rob left the room, put his protective gowning in a special trash container, and left the hospital. The bright sunlight made him squint. The heat of late August was already gearing up for another scorching day. He should be back on campus by now. Football practice had begun and the start of school was only weeks away. He'd talked to his coach. The team understood Rob's dilemma, but game strategy had to be planned. Rob knew he'd lose his starting position. He rubbed the base of his neck and slid wearily inside his beat-up Toyota.

He glanced at his watch. The date winked at him with an accusing flash. It was supposed to be his wedding day. Rob hunched over his steering wheel, closed his eyes, and expelled a weary sigh. He forced himself to ignore the sounds of the parking lot. All he remembered was the last conversation he'd had with Darcy. They'd sat in her car near a lake. The moon had been full and the color of ivory . . .

Darcy said, "Rob, I don't want to postpone our wedding. The invitations are printed.

Relatives are coming from as far away as California . . ."

He stared at her, seeing her beautiful face bathed in moonlight that reflected off her silken hair. "I can't believe you'd even think about a wedding when my sister's *life* is hanging in the balance. By late August, she'll be trying to recover from the transplant operation. She can't be a bridesmaid, she'll still be in the hospital."

Darcy reached out and touched his hand. "Rob, please try to understand my feelings. I know how difficult it is for you to think about our wedding at this time, but *try!* I'll replan the ceremony. Make it simpler and less formal. I've already bought my gown . . ."

"Maybe we need to rethink everything, Darcy," he said, swallowing hard.

She looked stricken. "You mean call it off? Oh, Rob! I don't want that."

"Somehow—whenever I think about Dawn's bone marrow transplant versus our wedding—the scale keeps tipping in her direction. But it's more than changing the wedding day, isn't it, Darcy?"

Her glance was quick and stabbing, as if he'd unmasked her. "I hate all the sickness here," she confessed. "Every time I come . . . it's horrible. Your whole household revolves around Dawn's illness. I—I've never had to live around sick people before. I can't stand it, Rob."

"Dawn can't help being sick."

"And I can't help hating it. Of being afraid of it."

Darcy's eyes shimmered in the moonlight. He knew that they had come to a hurdle they would never be able to overcome. *Good-bye, Darcy. If only . . .*

"Are you asleep?"

The question caused Rob to jerk into the present and stare out his car window into Katie O'Ryan's bright blue eyes. "No. Just daydreaming." He tried to cover his embarrassment. Katie looked pert and cute in a pale blue pants suit that was also her uniform. Her red hair tumbled over her shoulders and he noticed a fine dusting of freckles across the bridge of her nose.

"I'm on break," she said. "I'm going down by the pond to have an early lunch. I have enough for two. Care to join me?"

Suddenly, he wanted to join her very much. "I eat like a horse," he warned.

"Good. There's plenty of grass to graze on down there." She shook a brown bag at him. "Also two sandwiches, two apples, and four brownies."

He got out of his car and fell into step next to her. They headed toward the small, blue-green pond on the hospital grounds where there were picnic tables and benches. "Why so much food?" he asked. "You don't look like you eat enough to keep a bird alive."

"I never know when I'll be able to grab a bite, so I pack plenty and nibble on it whenever I get the chance."

"But if you share it with me . . ."

She held up her hand to stop him. "I can get something out of the machines in the nurses' lounge. I'd really like to get to know you better, Rob. Dawn talked a blue streak about you before the transplant. She thinks you hung the moon, you know."

Rob hunched his shoulders. "I think she's pretty special, too."

"Here—sit here while that tree is still shading the table."

Rob swung his long legs over the bench and watched as Katie unpacked the paper sack across from him. "I'm glad I'm able to spend some time with you also," he said. "I've been wanting to say thanks for all the extra attention you've given Dawn. I know it's your job. But nevertheless, our family really appreciates it."

Katie took a bite from her sandwich and laid

it onto her napkin. "Dawn's a very special girl. She has more courage and guts than I've seen in most adults. As a nurse, they train you to not become emotionally-involved with your patients. But I can't help it. I'm involved."

Rob studied the slim woman, seeing the softness in her eyes, hearing the compassion in her voice. "Thanks anyway."

"You did a brave thing, too. Offering your bone marrow."

Rob scoffed. "What worried me is that it might not be good enough. What if she rejects it, in spite of all the drugs you're giving her?"

"Rejection between incompatible donors is a very real threat. But so far, that's not happening. You can't assume the guilt if it does."

Rob shook his head. "I can't help it. I feel responsible for the transplant succeeding. Maybe because I want it to succeed so badly." He toyed with his sandwich wrapper. "Anyway, I hate hospitals. Somehow I see them as institutions of dying, not healing. Having Dawn walk out of there would change my opinion in a flash."

Katie nibbled on her apple. "Most people do come to the hospital to get well and go home. Dawn's a very special medical case. We're using technology that's very new.

Patients like Dawn are forging new frontiers for tomorrow's leukemia victims."

"I wish someone else could forge frontiers. It's frustrating. With all those medicines and machines and doctors . . . every day I expect her to get better. To get well. But she doesn't." He leveled a challenging look at Katie and asked, "Will she?"

The red-haired nurse took up the challenge in his eyes. "Rob, we're doing everything possible for your sister. Everything that can be done both medically and humanly. The human body is extremely complex. We can't ever give any guarantees. Right now, all we can do is wait. And hope."

Fourteen

DAWN hung onto life. The doctors became concerned about her heart. "It's under a terrible strain," Dr. Singh told the Rochelles. "We're keeping her attached to the heart monitor and I'm having a crash cart brought into her room in case she goes into cardiac arrest." Rob watched the green blips peak in the center of the screen that monitored his sister's heartbeat. He felt a sickening sensation in the pit of his stomach. Did they expect her to die?

Later, Rob asked Katie about it. "It's only a precautionary measure. Her reflexes are good and her heartbeat is strong. She does have periods of complete alertness and that's encouraging. As long as you hear that 'beeping' sound from her monitor, she's alive."

Rob wrote again in Dawn's diary.

Hi. They're planning to jump start

your heart if it takes a vacation. You know . . . like the time my car battery died and Dad had to restart it using special cables hooked to his battery. When you read this, you'll think it's crazy, but that's what they're going to do.

I can't wait for you to get home and see all the letters, presents, and junk your friends—Mom and Dad's friends too—have been sending you. I kid you not, Squirt. There's a pile of mail and packages a mile high in your bedroom. It'll take you a week to open it all. Your friends also call the nurses' station a lot. That girl Rhonda (she's nice, but sort of a bubblehead) phones every single day. Katie says that she sets her watch by Rhonda's daily calls.

Some boy called long distance from Cincinnati. I think his name was Jake or John. I'm sure you'll know who he is. Evidently news travels statewide via Rhonda—who is better than a daily newspaper about keeping your other friends informed. But it's good that so many people care about you.

So many are pulling for you, Dawn. So many . . .

Prickly sensations ran up Rob's spine. He felt as if someone were watching him. He glanced over to Dawn's hospital bed and stared straight into his sister's wide-open green eyes.

Rob knocked over his chair getting to her bedside. "Dawn! Are you awake?"

"Where have I been?" she asked. "I'm starved."

He rang for Katie, who came in on the run. "How are you feeling?" Katie asked, taking Dawn's pulse.

"Tired."

"You've been asleep for days," Rob said.

"I have? Like Rip van Winkle?"

Rob grinned. "Like Sleeping Beauty."

Dawn turned her head with great effort. Her voice was a whisper. "Where's my prince?"

"Turned into a frog and hopped off."

"Figures."

She improved as the days passed. Dr. Singh called for another bone biopsy and thought he findings spectacular. "Everything's looking good," he told the family. "We may send her home in a week to ten days."

The news encouraged Dawn so much that she told her mother what clothes to bring to the hospital for her to wear home. She refused to look into a mirror, knowing that it would only depress her. She remembered when she'd come out of intensive care during her first stay in the hospital over a year before. The image in the looking glass had been horrifying. No, she'd wait awhile. Maybe when she returned home and could put on some makeup . . . . Her mind whirled with plans.

Two days later, late in the evening, she began to run another fever. Outside, in the hall, Rob pounded the wall with frustration. Katie let him get it out, then asked, "Feel better?"

"Why? Why, when everything was going so good?"

"We don't know, Rob. But we'll attack again with antibiotics . . ."

"Stop it!" He shouted. "I hate it! First, hope. Then, no hope. Then, hope again. And now . . ."

"You must never give up hope," Katie cautioned. "Never."

A misty film coated his eyes. "I know."

Katie flashed him a broad smile. "Come downstairs with me. It's time for my supper break."

Rob hesitated, then decided that being with Katie was what he wanted and needed. In the hospital cafeteria, they chose a table in a corner and since it was so late, few people were in the big dining area. Rob surveyed Katie's dinner tray with dismay. "You're eating that stuff?"

"When you're hungry enough, even *swill* looks good." Katie laughed. Rob realized that she was really very pretty. Not a beauty like Darcy, but wholesome and fresh-looking.

"Dawn told me that you're engaged," she said. "So when's the wedding?"

"We called it off."

Katie's fork paused in mid-air. "Sorry. I wasn't prying."

"Dawn doesn't know. She'll think it's her fault because of the transplant and all. I don't want her to feel that way."

Katie eyed him, as if weighing her words. At last she spoke. "Rob, you once told me that you'd feel responsible if Dawn's body rejected your bone marrow."

"I still feel that way," he said stubbornly.

"And yet you don't want her feeling guilty over your broken engagement."

"That's right."

"Your logic doesn't wash, Rob Rochelle." Katie's smile was kind, her expression gentle. "Don't you see the conflict? How can it be your fault if the transplant fails if it's not her fault you're not getting married?"

Rob opened his mouth to protest, but

couldn't dispute her wisdom. He gave her a sheepish look, then confessed. "Okay. So I'm not logical." He hunched over. "Actually, the engagement was a bad idea from the start. Football star, prettiest girl in her sorority . . . two people need more than that," he added half under his breath.

Katie took a last sip of iced tea and glanced at her watch. "I have to get back to the floor."

They rode the elevator in silence. Katie's comments made sense and they gave him a lot to think about. At the door of Dawn's room, he said, "Thanks for letting me cry on your shoulder."

"I didn't mind." Katie touched his arm. Rob thought about hugging her, but decided it wouldn't be proper. She was just being kind. Why hadn't Darcy been more like Katie? "I'm going back into the room with Dawn," he said.

In the dimness of the room, he heard Dawn's shallow breathing along with the rhythmic beep of her heart monitor. Other equipment lined the walls. He heard Dawn ask, "Rob? Are you here?"

"Right here." He took her frail hand gently. At least she wasn't hallucinating as she had during her last bout with fever.

"I have a favor to ask." Her voice was soft and she spoke with effort. "I want you to pack up all my teddy bears and bring them here to the hospital."

For a few moments the impact of her request didn't reach him. Finally, he asked, "All of them?"

"Every one of them."

Cold snaked through his insides. "Even Mr. Ruggers?"

"He's so old and raggy, maybe you'd just better throw him away."

"Could I—Would you mind if I kept him?"

A partial smile formed on her mouth. "You're too big for teddy bears. But if you want to, you can keep him."

"Dawn. Why are you doing this?"

"I'm so tired." Rob had to lean over her to hear her words.

"You can't give up, Squirt." He heard his own voice catch.

"Rob . . ."

"You must fight, Dawn!" He interrupted. "You can't give up."

"I love you, Rob." Her eyelids closed. Next to her bed, Rob heard the steady beep of the heart monitor turn into a loud whine. He stared, open-mouthed, at the screen where the sharp peaking line had gone flat.

Fifteen

THE room erupted into a violent whirlwind of activity. Rob shrank against the wall as doctors and nurses rushed through the doorway. No one was sterile. He assumed it didn't matter.

A team of technicians surrounded Dawn's bed. Bedcovers hit the floor.

"No pulse!" A voice yelled.

"I can't get a blood pressure!" Another shouted.

Rob trembled as the room seethed with medical urgency. Over all the activity rose the persistent whine of the heart monitor.

"Don't you want to see your new sister, Rob?"

Seven-year-old Rob tugged his baseball cap tightly on his head, shuffled his sneakers on the carpet and flashed his mother a sullen look. No. He did not want to see the squirming bundle

that had arrived from the hospital in his
mother's arms. He'd never asked for a sister.
Why'd they go get one?

"Come on, son," Mr. Rochelle urged. "She's a
real beauty."

Obediently, Rob sidled over to the sofa and
stared down at the baby wrapped in pink, lying
in his mother's arms. Mrs. Rochelle pulled back
the edge of the blanket and Rob forced his eyes
to peek at the baby. His breath caught in his
throat. He'd never seen anything so small and
fragile. Fine red-blond fuzz capped her head.
Her eyes were closed, her mouth pursed, the lips
perfectly formed into a bow.

"Here, sit next to me and hold her." Mrs.
Rochelle patted the sofa cushion next to her.

Rob wanted to protest, but was so mesmerized
that he meekly sat and accepted the doll-sized
infant. He stared at her, enthralled by her
perfection.

"We named her Dawn." Mrs. Rochelle said.
"Because she's so pink and soft. Do you like
that name?"

Rob nodded silently, unable to look away
from the baby. Tiny lashes, no longer than the
hairs on his watercolor paintbrush fringed her
eyes, and her nose was no bigger than his shirt
button. Ever so slowly Rob lowered his cheek to
nuzzle against hers. Her skin was soft and she

smelled of powder and baby lotion.

"Dawn," he whispered. Her feather-soft breath fluttered on his cheek and a warm tingling sensation spread over his body. His arms tightened around her small form and he began to rock and chant her name.

"Get the cart!" The machine next to Rob was yanked into motion and shoved over to Dawn's bed. Doctors attached electrodes to her bare skin. Rob clenched his fists, held his breath, and pressed tighter to the wall. The sound of his blood pounded in his ears, merging with the mechanical screech of the monitor until he thought his eardrums would explode.

Someone called, "Clear." Doctors and nurses stepped away from the bed and the cart. The air snapped with tension. The body on the bed twitched as electricity surged through it.

Rob held up a rattle, gave it a shake and baby Dawn broke into a broad, toothless smile. Rob rubbed her plump cheek and tickled her under her chin. The baby squealed and giggled, thrashing her arms wildly. She grasped the rattle and Rob shouted, "Mom! Come see what Dawn can do!"

He patted her head, stroking the new growth

of red hair. Dawn dropped the rattle and grasped Rob's finger. He laughed and the baby laughed with him.

A doctor barked, "No response! Let's hit her again." Rob had lost all feeling in his fingers. He was cold. Why was he so cold? The machine zapped and crackled and the body heaved on the bed one more time. The monitor sent out a weak, wavering blip. Rob caught his breath.

Katie pressed her mouth to Dawn's ear and shouted, "Dawn! Can you hear me?" She clapped her hands sharply, but the girl on the bed didn't respond. The nurse turned to Rob and commanded, "Call her. Keep calling her name."

"Rob, does your stupid baby sister have to follow us everywhere?" Jimmy Callahan complained.

Guiltily, ten-year-old Rob turned his back on the three-year-old toddler tagging along on the sidewalk behind them.

"Aw, she's just a kid, Jimmy."

Dawn hesitated, stuck out her lower lip, and turned pleading green eyes toward her brother. "Dawn come with Rob," she announced.

"Doesn't she know she isn't wanted?" Jimmy

turned and stamped his foot.

"Don't scare her," Rob commanded.

"Why not? She's bugging me." Jimmy darted at the little girl. Dawn froze, stepped backward, caught her heel on a crack and fell flat on her bottom. She let out a loud wail.

"Now see what you've done," Rob shouted at his friend. "You scared her and now she's hurt." He rushed over to his sister and gathered her in his arms. "It's okay. Don't cry." He stroked her red curls and nestled her against his chest.

"Aw, crybaby!" Jimmy called, his face beet-red. "She's just a crybaby."

Rob felt anger surge through him. Suddenly he wanted to punch Jimmy in the mouth. "Get out of here!" He commanded. "Just go away and don't come back! You're a crummy friend. Get lost!"

Jimmy retreated and Rob soothed his sister. She wiped her eyes with the back of her hand and said, "Rob. Dawn loves Rob."

He led her to their porch steps and sat with her until she stopped crying.

"Dawn!" Rob repeated his sister's name over and over in her ear. "Listen to me! Wake up! Please wake up, Dawn!" The words poured out. Where was she? Could she hear him? "You can't leave, Dawn. Do you hear me? You cannot leave!"

A doctor shouted, "We've got a heart beat!" The green line staggered on the monitor, rising and falling in uneven peaks.

"I've got a pulse and a blood pressure." Sighs could be heard all over the room. "That was close."

Perspiration poured off Rob's face. His knuckles were white from gripping the sides of Dawn's bed. He heard her moan and he sagged, feeling his knees give way. An arm went around his shoulders. Katie said, "We got her back. She heard you, Rob, and she came back."

His brain refused to comprehend Katie's message. "From where?"

"From death," she whispered.

* * * * *

"What happened to me?" Dawn asked. Over a day had passed since Dawn's brush with death. Finally, she was alert, fever-free and anxious to talk about what had happened to her. The heart monitor etched green electronic peaks and valleys across its screen. Katie adjusted valves on the various IVs attached to Dawn's arm while Rob held her frail hand. Dawn saw dark circles under his eyes.

"You had no vital signs," Katie explained.

"Was I—," Dawn struggled to get the word out. "Dead?"

"Yes, clinically. But with such sophisticated technology, with the machines we have today, the line between life and death is sometimes blurred."

Rob asked, "But she had no heartbeat. No pulse. I saw her die."

"You saw her body cease to function. But death doesn't happen instantaneously. It takes time for all body systems to shut down. And it can sometimes be reversed if we act quickly enough."

"What did you do?"

Dawn's question caused Katie to study her intently. Finally she explained, "It's important that we keep the brain supplied with oxygen in order to avoid brain damage. So we work fast to restart the heart and get the patient breathing again. You have a young heart, Dawn, and an incredible will to live."

"That's important?"

"Sometimes that's everything. You can't revive someone who doesn't want to live."

"Someone kept calling my name."

"I didn't know you could hear me," Rob confessed.

"I heard you. At first I just wanted to sleep,

but you kept calling to me. I felt like I was a long way off, but I wanted to answer."

Katie added, "Medically, once these patients' vital signs return, they're alive again. We have no explanations as to what has happened to them. Or of where they've been."

"I—I don't know either, but I'm glad the machines were able to help. I'm glad I'm still alive."

For a few hushed moments, no one spoke in the room. It was Rob who finally broke the moment. "And now that you are alive, you've got to think about getting well and staying around."

"The bone marrow reports are good." Katie's smile was filled with promise. "Your white count is up to 5,800, platelets at 55,000 and hemoglobin at 13.8. Those are excellent numbers."

Dawn let out a long sigh. It wasn't over for her yet. She still had to recover completely before she could think the magic word—*cured*. "I hope I don't get another infection."

Rob patted her shoulder. "You won't."

Dawn allowed her eyes to search his tired face and another set of questions came to her. Questions she already knew the answers to, but felt she had to hear him confirm. "There's not going to be any wedding is there?"

Rob puckered his brow and exhaled. "No, Dawn. Darcy and I are through."

"I'm sorry."

"It isn't your fault and don't you dare take the blame. It isn't anybody's fault really. It's just the way things are."

Dawn saw Katie from the corner of her eye, pretending not to overhear their private conversation. "I'm still sorry."

Rob's eyes twinkled above his mask. "What's the matter? You afraid I won't be able to talk another girl into marrying me?"

"Right. Who would be interested in *you*?" She jabbed at him playfully with her forefinger. "What do you think, Katie? Think we can find any takers?" Dawn noticed color creep up Katie's cheeks.

"I'll have to continue this deep discussion some other time," Katie said. "I'll see you two later."

She left and Dawn puzzled, "Did I say something to scare her off?"

Rob stared at the door for a few thoughtful moments. "No. I think she needed to go take care of sick people, not people who need to rest and recover." He added, "And I need to go home and sack out for a while. Mom and Dad are waiting in the other room."

Dawn knew that her hospital room was too

small for too many to crowd in at one time. She nodded at her brother. "Come see me tomorrow."

"I will."

"And Rob—if you think of it, could you bring Mr. Ruggers?"

"You mean you've changed your mind about tossing him out? He's mine, remember? You gave him to me."

Dawn blushed. "Just stick him in a paper sack and hold him up to the window at the door. And don't give me a hard time."

Rob laced his fingers through his sister's. "Just a quick peek," he told her. "Then I'll take him home and tuck him in to wait for you."

Dawn let Rob leave, closed her eyes and took a few deep breaths. The air felt wonderful flowing into her lungs. She was alive! She'd been through a miracle and *she was alive!*

For the first time in a long time Dawn began to think of the future. Of going to school, of seeing Rhonda and Kim and—maybe even some day—Jake. Then there was camp and Mike and Dr. Ben. Dawn began to count the months to her fifteenth birthday.

**Look for
Lurlene McDaniel's next book about
Dawn Rochelle,
*So Much to Live For:***

Dawn Rochelle's leukemia is in remission again, and she's feeling great. She's working as a counselor at a camp for kids with cancer—the same camp she once attended with Sandy. Dawn knows the kids at the camp need her, and she feels good being able to help them. But the camp also brings back many painful memories. Dawn feels she has so much to live for now. Wouldn't it be better to just forget about cancer and everything connected with it?